Always.

A Bryce W. Starner Novel

Acknowledgements

It has been the utmost joy, having found the ability to make these words seep out of my mind and down into the tip of my pen. Although primarily fictional, "Always." stands as a pillar of real-world influence, particularly the events and individuals that have molded me into the young man that I am today. Without the unwavering love and support I've been blessed with over the past twenty years of my life, by no means would any of this story have been brought to fruition. For this, I love you, and I thank you.

More so than anyone else in my life, my family, especially my mother, Missy, my father, Jeff, and my brother, Chad, has been the anchor to my ship. They've been the ink to my quill and the light of my life. I can only pray that one day I will find the right string of words to tell you just how much you mean to me. You aren't strictly my always—you're my forever, too.

To my friends back home in York, Pennsylvania, it's only fair for me to give all of you the credit you so desperately deserve. While there are far too many of you to name individually, I'm confident that each of you is well aware of the role you've played in making this dream of mine come to life. Never will I lose sight of the town that raised me and the brothers and sisters who have stood resolutely by my side since I was a kid. Growing up, writing was by no means a strength in my intellectual arsenal. The power of your friendships has gifted my writing the ability to blossom into a flower that continues to grow with each passing day.

As I'm sure you will come to find, the memories I've gathered while on the baseball diamond will forever be my fondest. The sport of baseball has presented me with a band of brothers and coaches that I will continue to love and respect until my days on this planet reach their end. Each and every one of you has taught me how to embrace teamwork, perseverance, and humility, leaving me with lessons that I look forward to sharing with my own children one day. I'm forever indebted to you all.

For my fraternity brothers in State College, Pennsylvania, I have never felt more honored than to join the ranks of your upstanding chapter. It's no secret that you are the reason I've made it to where I am today, plucking me out of the psychological abyss that I found myself in as a lost freshman back in 2015. It has been (and will forever be) a privilege to call myself your brother and friend. Seeing the strides we've been able to make in the ever-changing dynamic of Greek life at Penn State has warmed my heart to a greater extent than any of you realize. Intellectual Awareness. Social Responsibility. Integrity. Brotherly Love.

I would be remiss if I weren't to thank Penn State Football, the Kansas City Royals, the York Revolution, and the Atlantic League of Professional Baseball for blessing me with opportunities to grow as a young professional with lofty dreams. Your trust in my ability to improve your prestigious organizations—even in such a small capacity—has bolstered my self-confidence and has directly impacted my belief that this book would finally see the printing press. I promise to take what you've taught me and apply it throughout the entirety of my career in professional sports. Your faith in me has never gone unnoticed and I hope that I've made you proud.

Para todos los que se convirtieron en mis hermanos mientras estuve en la República Dominicana: Ustedes me han bendecido con la luz de su cultura y la radiación de su amor. Mis puertas en los Estados Unidos siempre estarán abiertas para ustedes y pido a Dios que sus sueños se conviertan en realidad algún día. Siempre tendrán un lugar muy especial en mi corazón por el resto de mi vida. Royals por siempre!

To my dearest friends at Penn State University and elsewhere, the laughs we've shared and the unbreakable bonds we've constructed over the past four years are but a mere fraction of what the future holds in store for all of us, moving forward. I thank God every day that our paths have converged on our voyage into "the real world." It will surely be a privilege to see just how wildly successful you will all become in the coming years as we venture through childhood's gate, shapeless in the hands of fate. May our lives but swell thy fame—for the glory!

I'd like to thank my congregation at St. James Lutheran Church for instilling in me devotion and glorification for Christ from such a young age. To Pastor Brenda Ferree, I have no doubt that this story will bring a smile to your face in that land above the clouds. We love you, we miss you, and we vow not to lose our grip on the sermons you shared with us throughout your time at St. James.

To my readers, you never cease to open my eyes to the beauty of life and all that it has to offer. It's thanks to you all that I've discovered the power behind the word 'Always,' and the confidence to share my story with the world. I'm truly humbled to have found an audience as supportive as you are, so early on in my life. I hope that the pages of this book swell your heart as much as you do mine. Thank you for your unmitigated love and selflessness throughout this writing process and beyond.

Acclaimed sports anchor, Stuart Scott, was once quoted as saying that "When you die, that does not mean that you lose to cancer. You beat cancer by how you live, why you live, and the manner in which you live—so live." To anyone who has ever undergone treatment for cancer or who has had someone near and dear to their heart slip away from the ravages of the disease, I extend my deepest sympathy. You cannot possibly expect anyone to understand the card you've been dealt or to relate to all of the pain that's been inflicted on you or your family. However, I propose a challenge—unearth something beautiful that cancer has graced you with. Whether it's a stronger appreciation for your own life, a special evening spent holding the hand of a cancer patient lying in a hospital bed, or maybe even the grueling battle itself, refuse to turn your back to it.

I'm a firm believer that God doesn't present us with anything that we're not fully capable of handling; He saves his toughest battles for His mightiest angels. You may have the wind knocked out of your lungs. You may collapse in dismay, bloodying your kneecaps. At the end of the day, love and hope are always worth the hardship and will guide you through to the light at the end of your struggles. Discovering your true self will forever be worth the risk. I encourage you, my beloved readers, to embrace the gift of life that you've been given. Love will tie the tourniquet around all wounds. The dawn of love will survive forever.

Always,

Bryce W. Starner

All of the proceeds from "Always."

will be donated to cancer patients

through Penn State THON and the

York Cancer Center.

Thank you again for your support.

In Loving Memory of William Starner

Part I

It didn't take very long for us to fall in love, but it continues to grow and develop into an emotion stronger than the pain it can entail—something that I'm admittedly not all that familiar with. I'm used to love plateauing and eventually diminishing, which I guess is what I feared above all else. With you, I'm not afraid, because this incredible feeling of absolute euphoria can't possibly die. I fall more and more in love with you every day, Liam. As we move forward in this relationship, I promise that we're going to complete every item on our bucket list. Someday, we're going to travel to Greece, I'm going to shave your head, and we're going to have that food fight we've always joked around about. I wouldn't want to do these things with anyone but you, and that's the absolute truth. Thank you for showing me that love isn't something to fear, but rather something to admire, hope for, and cherish. Thank you for breaking down the walls that I so desperately refused to tear down. And most importantly, thank you for giving us a chance. It's beautiful, the depth of our love being surmised by a simple word like 'Always.' It isn't just a word; it's a promise that there will always be a sense of love between the two of us. I love you, and I always will.

Yours,

Emma

As I fold up her note and stick it back into my wallet for what feels like the millionth time, I can't help but take notice of its tear-soaked lines and how they smear into little, eloquent waves that ripple and flow from one side of the crumpled notebook paper to the other. It's been almost sixteen years since Emma passed away, and each day seems to grow increasingly harder than the one before it, except for the afternoons where I gather myself and drive over here to sit at her gravestone, tucked into the far-left corner of Weaver Hill Cemetery. It's quite serene, really, the white dogwood leaves stacked inches thick, occasionally leaving a rare glimpse of the luscious, green azalea grass underneath. Nothing thrills me more than to see the shredded flower petals after a mowing, covering the ground with what at first appears to be a quilt of freshly fallen snow. In summer, I usually lay in the blanketed shade of the dogwood tree and recap my day, giggling at the events of my morning that left me with a fleeting memory of her, always doing my best to remind her that I still love her, never losing sight of what still lies true in my patchwork heart.

As autumn and winter have come and gone over the years, I've learned how to brave the cold, kneeling at the freckled, charcoal-colored granite of the gravestone and reminiscing on the days that we were blessed to share with one another. But on comfortable spring days like today, I bask in whatever outfit I'm wearing, feeling rejuvenated by the chilling breeze that brings me to my senses and reels me back into the moment, crouched down with my head in-between my knees. It's during times like this when I find my heart warmest, probably because it's the closest to Emma I can get.

We met nearly twenty-three years ago at a student council summit during the early weeks of summer vacation. The conference was held in Frederick, Maryland, only a 45-minute drive away from my hometown in Bethesda, and proved to be one of the most grueling weeks of my teenage life. Students from all across the state gathered to tack on yet another résumé builder for their college applications coming in the following year, and I'll unproudly admit to being one of them. By the second day, I had found myself longing for departure as the guest speakers rambled stodgily on about leadership traits which were already common knowledge to everyone in the lecture hall. When the proctors delegated us into workshop groups, imminent misery loomed over my head and my focus darted towards that night's Orioles game and what my mom had planned on making for dinner. I wasn't a picky eater by any means, but Lord knew how dejected I'd be to come home to either ham or tuna casserole on the table; thank you, but no thank you.

All of that was the case until I was assigned a seat next to Emma, a mere beautiful stranger to me at that time. Although sitting beside a breathtaking blond girl with the greenest of green eyes may seem like a dream come true to a less-than-handsome, chicken-legged high school chump, it made stealing glances way too hard to avoid. I remember wishing I had a vantage point from the other side of the table, nervous as to what all she was thinking about as she sat beside an acne-ridden nerd like me. It took every ounce of self-control not to blatantly turn my head sideways and check her out, sitting only inches to my left, but somehow, I managed to stay cool and collected. It took almost an hour of listening to painstaking lessons and speeches until I finally coughed up the courage to lean over and whisper some stupid joke about the lecturer, who had by that point had sweated straight through his peach-colored dress shirt, into the ear of the adorable spirit which I'd come to know as Emma Aparicio.

Amidst the monotone speaking, light snores from the two guys nodding off at the far end of our row, and the ruckus of other groups marching down the hall to lunch, I remember making small talk with her, learning that she too lived in Bethesda. She attended the Buford School, whereas I studied at Boddicker High. Unbeknownst to me, her aunt was actually the secretary in the front office of my high school. I had no idea, as she went by "Ms. Blair," which was the maiden name of Emma's late mother. Emma shared with me that her father was tragically killed in a car accident when she was only five years old, and that her mother passed away while giving birth to her younger brother, Robbie, later on in that very same year. Julie Blair, the younger sister of Emma's mother, took in both children and raised them by herself rather than letting them enter the foster system. How someone so confident and radiantly beautiful could claw their way through to the other side of such a troubled childhood still baffles me, but it all came together to shape her as the young woman who I would eventually fall head over heels for.

From the inception of our friendship on that brutal June morning, Emma made it known that she had absolutely no intention of dating someone again until she was well into her college years, given that she had had her heart broken a few times in the past and wasn't about to let it spoil the so-called "best years of her life." I quickly found out that the more time we spent together, falling into the oasis of fervor and excitement was seemingly inevitable. After a few short weeks, it was obvious how strikingly similar we found ourselves to be. As two student-athletes with strong moral compasses, even stronger senses of faith and family, and ridiculous career aspirations, Emma and I made one heck of a dynamic duo. All of this was a side note to the fact that we acted like yin and yang when we were together, finishing each other's sentences to the point where it was almost second nature. Clichés were something that we prided ourselves on, and we vowed to hold on to that "honeymoon" feeling for as long as we possibly could. It only took a handful of dates for it to become fairly clear that Emma was slowly but surely (against her own free will) developing feelings for me, growing fond of my family, and finding comfort in my arms.

I could tell by the way she laughed and how she gradually opened up to me, acting just as casual and goofy as I was. Jokes (that I knew weren't even funny) never failed to bring a cramp to her sides, making her giggle until she started to cough uncontrollably. She confided in me the truth behind her infinite number of insecurities and a lot of other things I would have never guessed about her and her life, much like her heartbreaking story of losing both parents so early on in her childhood. She would talk about her aunt and her brother for hours on end, making it evident just how much of an impact they had on her. According to Emma, it was the first time in her life that she ever truly felt confident in divulging those things to anyone other than Aunt Julie and Robbie; with me, "it was different." Like myself, she too was a listener. I could babble on incessantly, and her focus never left my mouth, even pretending to be interested in what I had to say when she was obviously bored out of her mind. Emma always put people and their personal issues before herself, and that was one of the hundreds of things I grew to recognize and love about just how special she really was. In the months to follow, we weaseled our way into the most unlikely of relationships, but truth be told, the actual reason our roads converged would surely prevail in the months and years to come.

Junior year came and went in the blink of an eye, with me growing unfathomably closer to Emma all the while. At that point in our story, I had already considered her to be my best friend, not just my girlfriend. I remember how privileged I felt as I began to discover my own little niche within her family. Robbie adored the game of baseball and was already being looked at by a few collegiate programs as a middle schooler. As for Ms. Blair, she was one of the most kind-hearted, hard-working ladies I had ever met. Her aunt even spent most weekends working for a cleaning service to earn some extra cash aside from her secretary job throughout the week.

It was in their home one evening, gathered around the living room table playing board games with Robbie and Ms. Blair, when Emma leaned over and whispered into my ear that if anything were to ever happen to her, she wanted me to promise to help take care of those two whom she loved dearest. Without hesitation, I looked back into the depths of those sparkly green eyes hidden behind a few stray blond hairs and said "Always," putting my hand on her knee and sharing a warm smile that she immediately returned. Reassurance smeared across her face, she went on to plant a soft kiss on my cheek before reaching down to take her turn in the game, hoping to widen her already commanding lead on the rest of us. Little to my knowledge, that promise would be one that I'd have to carry, over two decades from that board game on her living room floor. We'll get to all of that in due time.

✝

Emma had been juggling a hectic work schedule, a tedious academic course load, and weekly softball practices, which ultimately bogged down her attitude towards her entire senior year. It did, however, make her acceptance into Stevenson University's honors program that much sweeter, looking back on it all. When financial aid assets were figured out, and her eight scholarships were cashed in, yearly tuition costs were practically nonexistent, and she'd be studying at one of the best schools in the state of Maryland. Their club softball program even offered her a spot on their roster after seeing her play in a local tournament, which thrilled her even more. Emma was notified of her admission in the early weeks of winter, but I had to wait and ended up finding out sometime in the middle of my senior baseball season, towards the end of April if I remember correctly. I used to sprint out to the mailbox every night for months, eagerly awaiting that tightly sealed packet from the mailman, but when the papers finally came, it made the wait well worth it. Although unsure of how the cards managed to fold in my favor, I made it into the University of Maryland's business school, which meant I would be close enough to visit Emma on a fairly regular basis throughout the school year. I couldn't have asked for anything better at that point in my life. It was as if God Himself was putting together all of these pieces in my life, showing me just how amazing of a puzzle I had in front of my very own eyes.

Senior year concluded with the prestige of Emmy (a nickname used by Robbie and Ms. Blair that I eventually grew fond of) achieving honors status as one of the best academic students in her graduating class. Looking back, I like to think that I was a reasonably good student. My grades were just above average, I was a varsity athlete, and I tried to volunteer and get involved in the community whenever I had the chance. When all was said and done, I ended up finishing just outside of the top ten percent of the 250 students in my graduating class, and missed out on the chance to wear the fancy golden chords around my neck on graduation day, which means absolutely nothing in retrospect, but upset me quite a bit back then. I'll never forget cheering at the top of my lungs for Emma as she stood up at that podium on the night of her graduation ceremony to deliver a speech as senior class president. Sitting in that overly crowded gymnasium with the balloons and streamers dangling just feet above my head, I was on pins and needles, much more nervous for Emmy than she was for herself.

The mental image is still clear in my mind; I can see her smile and ecstatic expression as she glanced up at me, Robbie, and her aunt sitting up in the top right-hand corner of the gym. Robbie forgot his glasses, so we had to turn the car around right before we got there, explaining why our seats weren't the best. When Emmy began to preach about love and hope, talking about how each principle got them to where they were on that day, gowns and tassels waving back and forth with the blasting air conditioning, my heart swelled, and my eyes couldn't withstand a wave of tears. You could have heard a pin drop at any given second as she shared her message with the crowd, every eye and ear attentively focused on her as she smiled and motioned to all of her peers, sitting anxiously in the rows of seats before her. The room erupted in screams and roaring applause as she concluded her brilliant sermon with a profound, yet simple, "Always," before walking down the steps and taking her place in the second row, a pearly smile hidden behind the fringes of her tassels and a long curl of her beautiful blond hair. Still clapping thunderously, I whispered for only myself to hear, "Always."

The summer after our high school graduation still stands out as one of the best I've ever had. I spent my days slaving away at Johnson's Orchard about five miles down the road from my house, while Emma took advantage of a less hectic schedule and bumped up her hours working as a snack stand attendee at the local movie theater to almost eight hours a day. She was already laying the groundwork for what was sure to be a long, yet successful life. We were lucky if we were able to meet up at a nearby snow cone stand on our way home from work some days, but it gave us something to look forward to and to work even harder for. Based off of what I was making at the orchard, those nightly snow cones probably cost as much as an hour's worth of work for me, and maybe even more for Emmy. On the weekends, we'd pack up my truck and go adventuring to places like Calvert Cliffs where we'd sift through the sand for hours on end, looking for sharks' teeth and fossils from the Chesapeake Bay. Sometimes we'd venture into Baltimore and go to Orioles games, sneaking two jumbo hot dogs from a food cart into the stadium, knowing how much more it'd cost us broke college-bound kids, once we made it inside the gates of Camden Yards.

It was on one of those thick and humid summer nights where Emma and I found ourselves drifting about the Chesapeake on my dad's rickety pontoon boat, which by that point was no less than twenty years old and hardly functional. The brackish water and sea algae had eaten away at the top coating of paint on the engine, leaving its metal worn down and cracked, no longer protected from natural elements. The crabbers went about their business, hauling in the final pots of the evening and taking pleasure in slinging the left-over bait out into the murky water, much to the delight of the flocks of seagulls tailing the wake of their boats. As the sun slowly stooped below the crest of the horizon as if it were trying to hide from the blanket of stars, there lay Emma and I on the pontoon floor, her head tucked into my chest and our fingers interlocked in the tightest of grips.

Amidst our giggles and star gazing, Emma's face suddenly contoured into an expression of sheer self-pride, and her smug grin spanned from ear to ear. With lips remaining sealed, every one of her mannerisms begged for me to ask what the deal was, or why she all-of-a-sudden came across as so sly and cunning. At first, I felt inclined to keep my eyes aimed towards the stars just to tease her and prolong her anxiousness, but I only managed to hold off for a minute or two before caving and asking about the epiphany that was dying to escape the confines of her silent mouth. As expected, Emma brightened up nearly as much as the stars above us and blurted out "A list! A list, we need to make a list!" "A list of what, groceries?" The look of annoyance that followed was almost enough to make me pee laughing. "No! A list for us to do together, like a bucket list, but for us to complete with each other. From exciting and adventurous to simple and intimate, cheap to expensive, stretching from our backyards to the farthest parts of the world, it'd have everything we've ever talked about doing. You know, like the cute ones they talk about online and stuff."

The excitement in her voice was palpable, and from that moment forward, I knew without a shadow of a doubt that it wasn't going to be some silly, careless idea of hers. Emma knew that if it were to be taken seriously, we'd both be tested, and the magnitude of our affection for one another would shine brightly in its truest colors. She didn't just want us to discover more about who we were as individuals, but instead, who we were as a couple and as two best friends. I try to look back on the trials and memories of that list every single day and smile for this very reason. Everything that Emmy and I did together, from that point on, was done out of love. And because everything on that bucket list was done out of love, everything was well done.

So, there we lay, scribbling away on the back of an expired boat registration packet with a half-broken pencil that we came across in the gunnel. Making sure not to rip a hole in the paper, I loosely gripped the grimy pencil and gently started to leave a trail of graphite that started at the top and made its way all the way down to the bottom. It began with a simple endeavor—a food fight. Anyone who was lucky enough to know Emma would have chuckled because it was right up her alley. If it came down to her either having food or me, I know she wouldn't have had to think twice! As we tacked on minuscule feats like "commentating people's actions at the grocery store," our list gradually evolved into more monumental bullets, the biggest of which was an overseas voyage to Greece. It was a place that Emma had only ever dreamt of visiting since she was a little girl and learned about it in one of her elementary school geography classes. Santorini, Athens, and Mykonos topped the list as we slowly built our way up from the feasible to the nearly unattainable.

As the hours came and went, we laughed hysterically and allowed our minds to venture both to and froe on the maturity spectrum as we compiled a guide towards how we'd live out the remainder of our relationship and, for that matter, the rest of our lives. By the time we got back to the dock, and I finally checked my phone, my inbox must've been twenty to thirty messages deep from my worrisome dad, begging and pleading for a status update on his beloved (piece of trash) boat. I smirked before turning off my phone to add to his suspense as I attached the hitch of the boat trailer to the back of my truck and crawled into the front seat where Emma sat, feet up on the dash and head slumped against the window. Even asleep, the slight upward curve of her lips brought a smile to my face, too.

The weeks to follow are best described as a blur, consumed with college shopping excursions, spending hours on end at work each day, and having quality time with both Emma and my closest buddies prior to everyone leaving for their universities in the earliest weeks of fall. Above all else, time was occupied by the pursuit of crossing off everything on our list, one by one. I remember the first "mission" as if it were only yesterday. Emma and I climbed into the truck and drove to a small grocery store on the outskirts of Bethesda, where a series of comical narrations soon followed, leaving us both in stitches and heaving from laughter. We filed in and out of each aisle, commentating the lives and shopping decisions of the disgruntled, hoggish, and freakishly unsanitary looking customers scanning the shelves in search of everything from saltine crackers to tampons. We turned quick-paced shopping cart pushes into the final leg of a 1000-meter relay in the Olympic Games, whispering loudly to one another in a broadcaster tone of voice, as the single mother of two slowly began to expand her lead on the elderly African American gentleman, who was slowly losing ground as he stopped to analyze which cereal box he wanted to drop into his cart. In case you're wondering, the mom ended up winning—go figure.

A personal favorite of mine was the time I surprised Emmy with tickets to the Dark Before Dawn concert in Baltimore at the Ram's Head, a small venue that made our front row experience that much cooler. For years, she had been a massive fan of theirs; even the band's hiatus over the past few years couldn't have lessened her love for their music. I picked her up later in the afternoon that day, convincing her that we'd be going to a local music festival at the Inner Harbor where a handful of small, unpopular bands would be playing along the pier for anyone who was willing to lend their ears. When I read online that the lead vocalist of Dark Before Dawn, Brooks Thorne, had reassembled the band and was heading back out on tour for the first time in years, I had no choice but to snag a pair of backstage passes for the two of us. "Seeing Dark Before Dawn in concert" was quite a far-fetched and lofty goal on our list, because when we wrote it down, the band was practically in shambles and no one knew whether they would ever record or perform music again. I was scared to death that she would find some hole in my secret plan because, well, she was Emma.

My nerves began to act up as the look of confusion began to spread across her face when we pulled into the parking garage of the venue, which was a little farther of a parking spot from the Harbor than she was expecting. After hopping down four or five flights of stairs to the ground floor near the Ram's Head, we strolled hand-in-hand up to the box office entrance where I revealed two laminated passes from my back pocket and flashed them at the short, stocky bouncer with a thick plastic earpiece. His jet-black sunglasses and bulging muscles were intimidating enough, so when he grunted and snatched the passes out of my hand, I flinched immediately. He returned the laminated VIP passes to me and motioned for us to follow him as he led us on a trek through the hallways and confusing passages that made up the staff-only confines of the facility. By this point, Emma had begun to fret, asking me "Do you know this guy? Why are we here? Is there something you aren't telling me? What are those—" as she desperately snatched for the passes in my left hand. Almost instinctively, I raised them above my head, smirking, as it was a lost cause for her petite 5'6" frame.

We passed storage rooms stock-full of amplifiers and electronic equipment before finally reaching two large, black doors at the end of the hallway. The bouncer tapped on the door four times with each hit evenly spread apart and somewhat louder than the one prior. Scared beyond words, Emma gripped onto my shirt and nestled herself behind me, frightened at what was lying behind that door. Emerging from the other side was a tall, lean-looking man who I assumed to be a tour manager. He welcomed us and asked us to follow him, looking quite concerned at the look of uncertainty and skepticism on Em's face. Fortunately for her, the suspense would only last another thirty seconds or so. The gentleman directed us to the door at the back of the room we were in, which was littered with guitar cases, chords, and a dozen roadies configuring amps, foot pedals, guitars, etc. When the final door was pushed open, the look on her face was worth every penny I had spent on the surprise. Emma's eyes were not much smaller than the size of softballs, and her jaw couldn't have been more than a few inches off the ground, gaping in awe at Brooks and the rest of the band, sitting in a circle of chairs, chatting nonchalantly and messing around on their phones.

Emmy looked up at me, stuttering and slurring her words in a pitiful attempt at trying to either thank me or ask me yet another question. Smiling (and feeling like the best boyfriend of all-time), I reached into the pocket of my ripped-up jeans and withdrew a pen and the expired boat registration slip. I clicked the pen and drew a thin, black line straight through the bullet about seeing the band perform, before sliding the list back into my pocket and leaning forward to kiss her directly in the center of her forehead. I whispered, "You should probably go over and say hello or something before this gets any more awkward," and winked before grabbing her by the shoulders and spinning her around so that she was facing a smiling Brooks Thorne, accompanied by four of her other biggest girl crushes. "Hey, sweetheart! How are you?" Brooks said as he made his way over to hug my star-struck girlfriend. I couldn't help but laugh at the paralysis of excitement and speechlessness that plagued every vein in her body.

As those two made small talk, I made my way over to the other band members to shake their hands and thank them for the opportunity, telling them that it was an experience I couldn't pass up, and how much of a dream come true it was for Emma. She eventually skipped her way over to hug and pose for pictures with the other musicians, trying her best to make them feel just as loved as her idol, Brooks. On our way out, the drummer slid us an autographed drumstick, a vinyl signed by the entire band, and a guitar pick. I didn't know if it was a part of the VIP deal, but hey, I wasn't complaining! Making our way down the stairs to the floor of the general admission standing section, she looked up into my eyes and said "Always," as she reached up and kissed me softly on the lips. Seeing her so happy and over the moon made me feel light on my feet and light in my heart. They rocked the house down and even sang our favorite song, which we sang (horribly) word-for-word. It was one of the best nights of her life, and one of mine, too. It wasn't just "another item off the list," but instead a memory that was sure to stick with me for the rest of my life.

The first semester of my freshman year was the farthest thing from a breeze. The first two full months consisted of aimlessly meandering around campus and getting acclimated to the college way of life, persisting my way through a rigorous academic schedule, and most of all, suffering through the agony of weeklong droughts without being able to see my best friend, Emma. The transition was one of the hardest things I've ever had to do, leaving my friends and family behind so I could be thrown into an unknown world, one lonely soul in a school with tens of thousands. I spent countless nights by myself, streaming baseball games on my computer and refusing to do anything other than wallow in my own self-pity. I hadn't experienced depression to that extent before, which made the drastic fall-off hurt that much more.

I had nobody. Emma had her club softball team, and her popularity seemed to carry straight from high school to college. I felt so happy for her, but pretty jealous, too. In passing by fraternity row on one Tuesday in late September, my head bent downward as I counted the cracks in the sidewalk, being approached by anyone was the last thing I was expecting. There were two guys who looked like upperclassmen sitting on a weathered and ripped-up couch on the front lawn of a house with three big 'ΦΣΔ' letters hanging above the front door. They waved me down, and I slowly made my way over to them on the far side of the yard after hesitating for a few awkward seconds. They introduced themselves as Rich and Tippy, and extended an uncomfortably-timed handshake, which I reluctantly shook. I thought it was a joke at first, their slightly unusual names, but I just went with it.

"You're going to walk into someone if you keep strolling with your eyes pointed at your toes, homie. You good?" chimed in Tippy before Rich added "Take a seat, man" and patted the torn cushion in-between the two of them. I struggled in deciding what to say, if anything at all, before spilling the story of my pathetic start over the first few months at UMD. I told them how I finally fell into a routine of cowering in my room for hours on end, refusing to eat more than once every other day, and feeling the constant urge to get in my car and drive home every weekend because that was my "safe place." Walking alone was the least of my worries, but I guess that just happened to be what caught their attention. The whole time, I could feel their genuine concern about what I had to say and how I felt, which was odd because to them, I was just a scrawny freshman walking alone down their front sidewalk no less than four or five minutes ago.

They both encouraged me to give a sincere effort at getting involved with some organizations on campus, and even extended an invite for me to come out with the two of them and the rest of their fraternity that same Friday to grab a bite to eat and catch the Nationals game in D.C. Humbled by their offer, I gladly said yes, and the rest of that week couldn't have gone faster. I was so grateful for the chance to watch my favorite sport in an atmosphere other than on a laptop in my dorm room. I met up with them at the same spot outside their house and was introduced to forty of their other brothers, all of whom were surprisingly sociable and welcoming. I had never heard of a fraternity being anything other than a bunch of older college guys who got drunk, did drugs, and practically tortured each other during initiation processes and stuff. I could tell that this group was pretty far off from that general stereotype, and I wasn't intimidated at all. We had a wonderful time, and I got the chance to talk to just about everyone, most of them expressing a mutual interest in learning more about who I was, what I was planning on studying, and where I came from.

At the end of the night, the Nationals wound up taking a 4-2 victory over the Giants, much to the delight of all the brothers, whose voices were hoarse from screaming at the right fielder the entire game, throwing back drinks, and singing along with the crowd in-between innings. Returning to campus, Tippy and Rich pulled me off to the side of the driveway and told me how much of a pleasure it was, and that they would be honored if I were to consider joining their brotherhood and becoming a member of Phi Sigma Delta. I was so stoked for the opportunity to have a group of close friends at college and actually have people to confide in, especially when I didn't have Emma right there by my side. Soon thereafter, I began the casual rush process before accepting their bid invitation. I was formally initiated a week or two after their brotherhood unity period was completed, and I still look at it as the single most influential blessing towards helping me survive college. Much like Emmy, I don't know where I would be today if I didn't have all of them to take me by the hand during that rough time in my life. In a sense, they filled the shoes Emma couldn't while she was away at Stevenson, and their unconditional support was perhaps my biggest saving grace in my home away from home.

When it came down to making trips to Stevenson to watch her play, I somehow managed to always make it out on top after battling beltway traffic and horrendous construction. In balancing my class schedule and Phi Sigma Delta functions, I made almost every single one of her home games and an occasional road game, too. Very few things at that time in my life, and still to this day, compared to our post-game kisses with my lips caked over with green body paint and my voice sounding prepubescent from all of my screaming with Ms. Blair, who made it to as many games as her two jobs allowed.

✝

I'd be lying if I said that after all of these years, our college sleepovers didn't distinguish themselves as some of my favorite memories, not just memories of my time spent with Emma. Whether we found ourselves cuddling on the top bunk (which we were thoroughly convinced would collapse at any given moment) watching illegally-streamed movies off of the internet or strolling down the main stretch of campus, I refused to take any second of it for granted. My eyes didn't have to be open to feel the warmth and loving emittance as she lay slumbering by my side, much like the beams of sun that shoot through the canopy of dogwood leaves here at Weaver Hill Cemetery. One weekend in early December, I found myself snowed in when Emmy and I awoke on that Sunday afternoon. According to the local meteorology team, it looked like I would be stranded there, at Stevenson, for another day or two at least. Lord knows I couldn't tell my parents or I'd get the whole "We're paying for you to go to class, not miss it because of going to see your girlfriend," scolding from my mom or a lesson about not putting myself in a situation in which I would have to drive when the weather sucked so badly.

Given the fact that my homework was done, and I still had an extra change of clothes for the extended stay, we had the brilliant idea of snuggling up to scratch off one of the most time-consuming endeavors on our couples' bucket list—a nonstop marathon of The Office, our favorite TV show that we'd already watched together from beginning to end. I mean, we couldn't have asked for a more perfect situation, looking back on it. Finals were about a week and a half away, so studying commitments wouldn't allow for us to spend any more time together until Christmas.

So, there we were almost a day and a half later, our eyes crusty and strained from our refusal to sleep until the credits rolled around after the closing scene in the fourth season. I kid you not, the second that 24" television screen turned to black after the final episode in the series, Emma's eyes were closed, and she was well into her world of slumber. I carefully crawled over her, climbed down the bunk ladder, and walked over to my wallet which was sitting on her desk. I pulled out our list and then a ballpoint pen from her top drawer. I scribbled out the "The Office marathon" bullet point, which was so much more liberating than I could put into words. I slid it back into my aging wallet, and jumped up onto the top bunk before tucking myself underneath the covers and an extra layer of blankets so that I was right beside my best friend. I could see the snowflakes fall as I stared at the cracks between the window blinds.

With little to no surprise, Emma rounded out her spring semester and first year at Stevenson on pace to become magna cum laude of her class, while I settled in with a comfortable 3.54 overall GPA. Dad got a new job at a small insurance office late that spring, and my family relocated to Lutherville. I spent the first twelve weeks of that summer on a trip abroad to a small university located outside of Boca Chica in the Dominican Republic. Unbeknownst to me, the agony of not being in constant contact with my family and Emma soon sent me into a full-blown state of depression, yet again, not even two days after my arrival in the land of the palm trees and sandy beaches. Nearly every day of the trip was spent viciously banging the screen of my outdated and tattered iPad in hopes that it would restore the Skype connection with Emma and my family, who were still trying to accustom themselves to their new home.

I'd try my best not to express any hint of sadness to Emma, so as to not make her feel any worse about the long-distance situation, but some days were significantly harder than others. Behind those fake smiles and rough webcam connections laid welling tears and one heck of a broken heart. But sure enough, the time flew by, and along with my newly established Spanish fluency, back to the U.S I went. If I could convey to you the emotion of that hug in the airport terminal from Em, I would. After all these years, I'm still struggling to find the right words to describe it. The first word to escape my mouth and float into her ear during that overdue embrace was "Siempre." She didn't have to understand Spanish to know what it meant.

Our sophomore, junior, and senior years flew by as a blur. Emma excelled both inside and outside of the classroom, earning her accolades in softball and graduating twentieth in her class of almost 1,000. Johns Hopkins was practically on their hands and knees begging for her to enroll as a graduate student, expecting the same success and achievement that she boasted while at Stevenson. It was both an honor and a privilege, so without hesitation, she accepted an offer of admission into their medical school program early that spring. I, on the other hand, found myself stuck between two corporate offers based out of Baltimore—one for Johnson & Johnson as a low-level pharmaceutical representative and one for Under Armour as a professional development coordinator for the Central American branches of the company, due to my fluency in Spanish. My mom's innocent reaction was priceless, laughing hysterically at the fact that my offer from J&J would be based around me selling drugs; as a relatively innocent guy, it was admittedly pretty weird to look at it that way. Thinking long-term, I surrounded myself with the thoughts of my time spent studying abroad and how much I missed my family and Emma. I came to the realization that if I were to embark on this new journey into adulthood while in a serious relationship, then I couldn't afford to be thousands of miles away from the places and people that I cared for with all my heart. With that, I happily accepted the position at J&J and fulfilled my dream of starting out life in "the real world" with a respectable salary and a job that kept me so close to home.

Very few words can describe the pure exuberance of living with Emma. It took us a few weeks into the summer following graduation to find a small villa on the outskirts of Baltimore, where we took the far-from-spacious one room, one bath, and one kitchen living quarters (that we always drew in comparison to Harry Potter's cupboard underneath the stairs) and made it our own. I remember weekly trips to the outlets and home décor shops, in search of homey decorations, lights, candles, and picture frames to liven up our first shared living space. We'd never cease to amaze visitors with our brilliantly designed, small-scale "pad." I always joked around about getting in touch with one of those home modeling magazines for them to do a write-up on our place, but Emma always talked me out of it. Our efforts towards checking off objectives from the list hit a little bit of a stand-still at that point in time, but soon thereafter, we held our nose back to the grindstone and worked swiftly on eliminating bullet after bullet on the list with things like "go to a drive-in movie," "learn how to drive stick shift," and "try learning how to speak Swahili." It's safe to say that the first two were significantly more doable than the third, but we gave it our best shot! Life as we knew it seemed to be more of a fairytale love story than anything else—until her lower back pain began.

It started off as mild irritation and discomfort, leaving Emma wincing from time to time, typically when she'd bend down for something in the kitchen or when she'd try to unload groceries from the car. Being the resilient and stubborn woman she was, the popping of two Advil and sleeping with a heating pad at night were enough to subside the pain, at least according to her. Come time for her classes to start, she'd practically be crawling through the door every evening with an agonizing look spread across her no longer youthful face, exhaustion leaving not an ounce of strength left in her system. I remember the one time we returned from the store, I was outside at the truck, grabbing the last of the grocery bags when I heard a blood-curdling scream from inside the apartment. I sprinted up the steps, only to find Emma laying in the kitchen with an exploded gallon of milk splattered all over the floor. She claimed that she just stubbed her toe on one of the chairs around the kitchen table, slipped, and sent the milk flying, but I could see right through her fib.

I was well aware that her back was getting substantially worse, especially after seeing all of her toes looking fine as she walked down the hall to the bathroom with her back hunched over in the most uncomfortable of postures. She'd fallen into the routine of going directly to our room to nap for hours on end upon returning home, eating dinner late at night, and returning to the desolate confines of our room, dreading the burden of classes, driving, and homework in the day to follow. After urging her for almost two weeks, Emmy finally caved and allowed me to take her to the chiropractor to assess the source of her lower back pain. I was convinced that it had gradually climbed higher up her spine, but she was too proud to admit weakness of any kind. I always emulated how strong she was, but in cases like these, being stubborn was flat-out unacceptable. With no clearly defined diagnosis, we turned our efforts to no less than five other practices and specialists, all of which came to no definitive result. Emma grew shockingly more emaciated and feebler with each passing day, and my heart filled with unfamiliar amounts of worry as I saw her appetite dissipate and the color in her cheeks disappear. I was dumbfounded at how a person of such lively nature and superb health could become so sick and pitiful in such a short period of time. It broke my heart to watch, and I had a gut feeling that this was the start of some sort of nightmare.

Upon our visit to yet another clinic, they suggested a CT scan and a biopsy to determine the source of the discomfort and to pinpoint what exactly the issue was. The days before our follow-up were spent sitting quietly at home, given that Emma was excused under medical leave from her studies. I had already begun to cash in my sick days and holidays, only a few short weeks into my first legitimate job. When the morning came, our fingers were tightly interlocked while in the office, much like that evening out on the Chesapeake, all those years ago, when we made our bucket list. The young, crew-cut physician eventually snuck into the room, failing to show a hint of a favorable look on his face. As he turned the computer monitor around, it was safe to say that the words to follow would fall upon two sets of deaf ears. The body projection was scattered with a wide array of colors and growth, both of which we didn't have to understand to recognize their severity. We sat in dead silence, fingers still interlocked, although not nearly half as tight as before.

The doctor went on to explain that Emma was suffering from the brutal effects of late-staged metastatic breast cancer. He defined the word "metastatic" as a way to highlight that the cancer had spread to the bone, explaining her excruciating spinal pain in the weeks leading up to that distilled moment. The plan of action was to begin intensive rounds of chemotherapy, injections, medications, and potential operations immediately. I felt like the love of my life, my best friend, was about to turn into a science experiment, and it tore me apart on the inside far more than I could ever begin to express in words. I remember the look on Emma's face; her once joyous expression had by then faded, and those green eyes weren't as green as they once were. It was as though the glimmer of those little bluish-green oceans had seeped away, leaving a dull grey that resembled the dark and ominous clouds of a summer storm. And much like a summer storm, my eyes, too, began to rain.

It was almost as if the car ride home was set into slow motion; the hopeless confusion and agony of the morning led the trees and the skyline to blur into one convoluted landscape. At first, we sat in complete and utter silence, staring aimlessly through the windshield and into the empty lanes of traffic that were sat out ahead of us. It took upwards of two days for us to gather the courage to pour out our feelings and our fears onto one another, both of which were strewn with floods of sobbing and choking on thin air. Never in my life have I cried as hard as I did that evening. To no surprise, Emma stood resilient, glaring back at me with those eyes that had finally returned to their green nature, perhaps more so than ever before. Wiping one single tear from the corner of her right eye, she said, "Liam, you're my rock. If we're going to give this cancer a run for its money, you're going to have to stay strong for me. Some days are going to be tolerable, and others will try to knock me down and keep me there, but we can't succumb to it all and give it the satisfaction of already knocking us to our knees when the battle has only just begun. Anything that we do together in love is well done, and nothing will ever change that. Do you understand?" I sniffled no less than thirty times, doing all in my power to mask the onset of tears welling in my eyes. But I slowly nodded, only to end the conversation with a whispered "Always," before reaching over to turn off the lamp sitting on my nightstand, rolling over to Emma's side of the bed, and burying my face deep into her chest so that she didn't have to see my tears flow yet again. That night, sleeping was an impossibility.

Emma's oncologist decided to start intensive rounds of chemotherapy immediately, which turned days into what felt like months, and weeks into what felt like years. As if it were yesterday, I remember our first conquered objective from the list following her diagnosis. It was less than four weeks into her treatments when the first clump of voluminous blond hair had detached from the top of her head and fell quietly to the shower floor. Rather than continuing to shampoo and pull at the other loose-ended strands that occupied the surface area of her skull, she merely dried herself off and slowly made her way into the bedroom where I lay, nearly half-asleep from all of my commuting earlier that same day, doing what I had to in order to keep my job. Although I took notice to the bald patch the second that she stepped out of our bathroom and into the bedroom, I kindly pretended not to notice it, in fear of breaking her heart even more. Reluctantly, she read me like a book and called me out from across the room, telling me to stop being ignorant and to stop pitying her. One thing about Emma that everyone remembers to this day was her dignity; she didn't feel a need for people to engulf their own well-being with the trials and misfortune that clouded her own life. If something was wrong with her, she always felt obligated to fix it herself.

After helping lift her into bed and wrapping her cannula delicately underneath her nose, I was puzzled (and quite frankly, scared) to see her pull out a glistening pair of scissors from the right-side pocket of her robe. Gently, she reached over to my side of the king-sized bed and tugged on my pajama bottoms, motioning for me to slide over closer to her. With brief hesitation, I rolled over, only to face a smiling Emma. It was the first time I noticed a genuine smile on her face since we were made aware of the status of her disease. She slowly nuzzled her middle and index fingers into the larger of the scissors' two holes, as her thumb comfortably slid into the smaller, more circular one, and began to reach above my nose, surpassing my eyes, until she finally reached to the top of my head and lopped off a handful of my thin, dirty blond hair. The first thought to enter my mind was something along the lines of, "Oh God, I can't go into work looking like this," but I tried my best to conceal my emotions before knowing for sure what Emma held in store, up the sleeves of her purple nightgown.

She continued to cut, quickly at first, then slower and more steadily as the hair from atop my head began to litter the bed sheets, which made for a horrible mess to clean up the morning to follow. She then turned the clippers onto her own head, and when all was said and done, there we sat in a bed that was ridden with hair, as bald as bald can be. We couldn't help but look back into the depths of each other's eyes and laugh at how ridiculously different we each appeared to be, baffled at how we made light out of a seemingly dark and disappointing stage in her battle. What happened next continues to stand as one of the most remarkable things I'd ever seen come out of Emma during her time of sickness. From the left-side pocket of her robe, she pulled out our list and a small, black ballpoint pen. When she snuck it out of my wallet was beyond my knowledge, but I decided not to question it. With a smile that never fleeted, she unfolded the crinkled paper and drew a hefty black letter "x" through the bullet that read "shave Liam's head." We burst into tears and held each other close, whispering about how much we loved one another and vowing not to lose sight of the little things we were able to share together. She leaned forward, eyes closed, and pressed her forehead to mine, taking me by the hand with as strong of a grip as she could muster. For the first time in what felt like forever, our tears were reflective of something special, something beautiful. In that moment, cancer did not win.

Similar to that dreadful car ride home on the day of Emma's diagnosis, the weeks following our appalling haircuts whizzed by as a blur, most days distinguished by the agony and perpetual sorrow of losing our grip on the world we once knew, and trying to find a grasp on the world that was becoming our reality. It was around that time when I made the conscious decision to no longer prolong the inevitability of fulfilling my teenage dream of asking Emma to spend the rest of her life with me as her husband. I remember having our next-door neighbor, Melvin Lee (a plump, kind-hearted fellow whom we jokingly assumed still lived with his mother down the hall), come over late one evening after I tucked Emma into bed to be there in the living room in case anything happened to go wrong with her oxygen tank while I was out on my quest to find the perfect ring with her aunt.

I wanted something reflective of what we shared, Emma and I—a ring that wasn't overbearing and fancy, but simple and captivatingly beautiful. It needed to be a ring that you could tell involved an unreal amount of concentration, patience, risk, and pure love in its making, just like our relationship. When I was starting to lose my patience at what had to have been the sixth or seventh jewelry store of the night, I found exactly what I always envisioned the ring to look like. The sleek, white gold band was perhaps the most perfectly circular ring of the bunch, encrusted with two rows of smaller diamonds which wrapped symmetrically around the band's outermost edge, only to be crowned with a diamond that was so immaculate in nature, it looked as though it belonged on the cover of a magazine. Although the price wasn't nearly as low as what we'd dealt with in the other shops we visited that night, I was more than willing to swipe the credit card and take it home that same evening with my contentment left unscathed.

I crept quietly through the apartment door and into the living room before waking up a snoring Melvin and sending him back to the comfort of his own bed, a few steps down the hall to the right. I crawled into bed, cuddling up beside my breathtakingly beautiful wife-to-be. It was an evening of rejoicing, but not having the typical "hair in the face" predicament to deal with every night while sleeping beside her hit me like a freight train, more so that night than any other time before. Falling asleep with tears flooding down the sides of my face and onto the anguish-soaked pillow cover was gradually turning itself into a pitiful expectation, night in and night out.

Only a few, short days after dishing out a quarter of my life's savings on a ring for Emma, I arranged for both of our families to show up at a beautiful outdoor restaurant called Ember. I wanted them to be there to experience both the proposal and marriage with us, all of which was unbeknownst to Emma, who now found herself in a wheelchair due to the course of her recent chemo sessions. Ember had the most beautiful gardens, man-made ponds with tiny flowing streams, and some perfectly placed lights that were strung elegantly all across the patios and gardens. This little taste of perfection seemed to take the spotlight away from the illuminated crest of Baltimore's hazy skyline glowing miles off in the distance. After a delectable meal of chicken parmesan and linguine pasta, I took hold of Emma's wheelchair and slowly pushed her into the center of the lavish garden, where a smiling huddle of those we loved the most greeted us with warm smiles and watery eyes.

Unaware of what was happening, she blurted out with as much energy as she could produce, "What the heck are you guys doing here? Why is everyone dressed so nicely? Aunt Julie, why are you crying?" With a subtle movement of her hand, Ms. Blair pointed her finger and motioned in the direction directly behind Emmy's aim of view to where I was kneeling, hopelessly fighting the vault of tears that tried so desperately to ruin the moment as I tightly pinched the ring between my fingers. When Emmy spun the chair around and saw me, she immediately began to bawl, coughing up "Always," before I could even ask her to be my wife. It was there, on that crisp, mildly-chilly fall evening, that the local pastor arrived and conducted the most informal of all wedding ceremonies. It was perfectly simple, precisely the way Emma would have wanted it to be, with our families there to share the moment with us.

Sure, we didn't have an extravagant reception or a cake to shove into each other's faces. We didn't have the voluptuous wedding gown and our best friends dressed to the nines standing beside us. The only thing that mattered on that night was us defying whatever cancer was "supposed to" take from us. After an exchanging of the most heartfelt vows either one of us could have ever prepped for, we said our "I do's," and kissed as passionately as we had in months. I slowly removed the cannula from underneath her nose, pressed my lips to hers, and held our foreheads pressed together just as we had a few weeks prior after bidding farewell to our hair. Since the inception of our friendship, I knew that Emma was my always. It was on this night, however, when I'd come to realize that she was my forever, too.

After another month of extensive chemotherapy, we were scheduled to sit down with the practice's most prestigious medical mind, Dr. Gregg Wilhelm, for Emma's six-month re-evaluation. Upon walking into his office, we were blasted with an overwhelming scent of peppermint Yankee Candle that failed pitifully at calming our senses as we looked around for somewhere I could sit and park Em's wheelchair. His undergraduate and graduate degrees hung in their dark, cherry frames above the equally-dark desk as if they were to highlight the king, sitting upon his medical throne. Wilhelm's solemn look as he entered the office and inspected the files sitting upon his desk was almost enough to make me throw up in my mouth, even before he spilled the news about what the paperwork and follow-up tests showed. Rather than addressing Emma, his vocal darts were aimed in my direction, as if he was too noble (or too embarrassed, even scared, maybe?) to express to her the cancer's resistance to the chemo treatment, hinting at a loss for any remaining options—hinting at a loss for any remaining hope.

Emma looked up at me from the sunken lap of her wheelchair, only to crack the most untimely of smiles. Whether she had challenged the thought for those past six months is still unknown to me, but in that moment, it was obvious that she had accepted the fact that she was going to die. I asked myself, "How could anyone possibly delve into the reality of something like that? How could she be so content with leaving behind all that she loves in this world so that she could fly up and live in the next one?" I remember being so unfathomably angry at her willingness to surrender to the disease and her refusal to fight until her very last breath. It was something that I wouldn't understood until many, many years later.

It was only a matter of time until God was going to beckon for her to come and join His army of angels amidst the clouds and the heavens. That was the last time for a very long while that I acknowledged any speck of belief in God. I just never understood how someone of such high praise could ever take everything away from a person as angelic as Emma. It just wasn't fair. Then again, wasn't He supposed to have a plan for our lives that was greater than our own dreams? He was a scam, a phony. Why I wasted so many hours in a chapel throughout my life was beyond my comprehension, because it apparently did no good. I was tired of pretending to believe in anyone or anything that resonated such unhappiness within the bounds of my heart. I was shattered on the inside and God was to blame.

It wasn't more than two weeks after that appointment that Emma's quality of life began to slope downhill at an increasingly rapid rate. Her days became shorter, typically occupied with endless hours of sleep, a loss of appetite, and an inability to communicate the way she always had. I'd sit there, holding her hand and watching her moan in her sleep from the discomfort in her back and her joints, almost to the point where I had to momentarily walk away to gather myself so I wouldn't lose my composure in front of her. Friends and family drove from all over the east coast to visit, saying goodbyes which would ultimately prove to be their last. Seeing her aunt and brother in so much pain and worry was something that haunted me—no one deserved to experience that much heartbreak, especially those who I called "family." No one deserved to suffer the agony of watching their niece or sister slip away, and although I was also in their shoes, it still sickened me to my core.

Hospice was invited into our home soon thereafter, leaving Emma in a cot in the living room for easier accessibility. Our bed fell into a permanent state of emptiness, as I slept out on the couch within an arm's length of my dying wife. It's often said that in the hours leading up to the end of the battle, cancer patients experience one last phase of painlessness, serenity, and happiness as if it were life's final gift of what it was like to feel healthy again. I remember Emma acting as though nothing were wrong and as if she had the energy to jump out of bed, make dinner, then start studying her medical school material again. She was cracking jokes, asking me about how I was feeling, and recounting funny memories that the two of us had shared together over the years. Her smiles stretched ear to ear, and we made thoughtful conversation for hours on end.

Before her head had hit the pillow that evening, she decided to remind me of my promise to take care of her brother and aunt, from all those years ago at her house when we were playing board games on the living room floor. "Liam, you need to promise me two other things. I need you to find love again; you deserve a relationship that will help lead you through the rest of your life, the good times and the bad times alike. I'm sorry I couldn't be that person for you, Liam. I'm sorry." The tears began streaming down my face as I nodded with reassurance even though I knew the only person who would ever have my heart was lying there in my arms, hanging onto life by a few short threads. "And lastly, I need you to promise me that you'll never lose your faith in God. If it weren't for Him, we never would have made it this far. The amazing memories, our struggles, and everything in-between has been because of Him. We owe it to Him for all that we've been able to live for, together, through all of these years. Our list would still be a blank sheet of paper in your dad's boat today if it weren't for God's plan, so you can't lose sight of that, Liam. Promise me this." Again, I slowly nodded, gripping her right hand in mine, using my other hand to wipe a lone tear from just below her eye as it raced down her cheek.

I looked deep into Emma's eyes, the oxygen concentrator beeping quietly from across the room. "Always, Emma. Always." As she closed her eyes, she whispered back "Always, Liam," with a small smile on her face, gently allowing her head to fall back onto the pillow as she drifted off to sleep. The quiet thumping of her heart and the soft breaths from her nose slowly lessened that night as she slept until they finally stopped altogether.

✝

Her funeral was on a Friday afternoon. The birds were uncharacteristically quiet, the wind was slightly less than breezy, and there wasn't a single cloud in the sky. We all gathered around the property on the back half of Weaver Hill, dressed in black. Friends, family, neighbors, and colleagues circled around her casket, lying beneath a handful of red and white rose petals that were sprinkled on by the pastor after every prayer read.

The number of people who turned out that day was astonishing and put into perspective how loved Emma was, so much so that the funeral home had to shuttle in over a hundred people who couldn't find space to park at the cemetery. I stood there, feeling alone in a crowd of hundreds, staring blankly at the six-foot pit at my feet. It was so hard to make eye contact with anyone who came up to me, shaking my hand or offering a hug of condolence. I couldn't even mutter a "thank you" or a nod of acknowledgement. As the pastor stepped up to the sleek, black, pearl-handled box beside the gravesite, the tears began to flow out of my eyes like a river. It took my dad and my brother to hold me back from rushing towards the casket and begging, pleading to let me see her one last time.

Everyone cast glances of disbelief and embarrassment at how I was acting and just how persistent I was at never letting go, almost like I was a child who had to let go of a parent. Had any of those people felt that way about someone before? So strongly that it felt like they've died, too? I smacked their hands away from me and ran to the white dogwood tree, hunched over and sobbing, my tears soaking the exposed roots and fallen flowers on the ground as the natural moisture from the soil soaked through the thin layer of material of my dress pants. I leaned my head against the sturdy base of the tree, traces of bark landing softly in my hair. I could feel the masses of eyes watching me, but I didn't care. I didn't care about anything anymore. I spat on the ground, cursing God for what he took from me and shunned Him for stealing my angel to have all for Himself. I was enraged.

I stood up, throwing my fists into the trunk, shrieking after every jab. The blood dripped from my knuckles, reddening the white coating of leaves covering the ground. I could feel it running down the back of my wrist, positive that it was staining my white cuffs and seeping between the links of my titanium watch. When my hands finally went numb with pain, I bowed my head and collapsed back to the ground, ashamed at what Emma must have been thinking of me from her new home up in the heavens. I could hear the footsteps of the guests slowly distancing themselves from the service area, walking down the beaten asphalt path winding its way through the field of gravestones. But there I sat, all by my lonesome. The sound of shovels scooping and sifting through piles of dirt, leaving hollow thumps as they landed on a nearby casket, made my stomach churn. The cemetery workers were long gone by the time I finally opened my eyes, coming back to my senses.

The sun had already gone down, and the sky was left in an ugly shade of gray. I stood, my eyes glued to the untouched heap of soil at the base of her tombstone. I knelt, taking a small handful and slowly pouring it back, my eyes fixated on the casket that was soon to be lowered into the cold ground beneath my feet. I felt a drop of rain on the back of my neck. Then a second. A third. My best friend and my soulmate, only hours away from being sent below the soles of my mud-covered shoes, and there I was, bloodied and drenched in the midst of a thunderstorm, well on my way to becoming a heartless recluse. Barely making out the distant image of two cemetery workers huddled under the canopy of a shed, waiting for me to leave, I collected myself and managed two steps towards the iron gates at the entrance before turning around and whispering, "Always." It was almost a question, as if I wasn't even sure of it anymore. I trudged through the puddles on the way down to my truck and pried open the bar to the cemetery gates without the courtesy to even close it.

I crawled into the driver's side and sat, watching the raindrops trickle down the windshield. I thought back to when I was a kid, watching intently to see which one would win the race and reach the bottom of the window first. I saw two of them converge, forming one big droplet. "That was supposed to be us," I said out loud to myself. Together, one force. One big entity that was destined to change the world and help the people in it. I stuck the keys in the ignition and started the truck. By then, the rain had picked up drastically and seeing five feet ahead of me was an impossibility. I was so tempted to just put it into gear and floor it, not caring about what I would crash into or what harm I could do to myself in the process. But just as I put my hand on the shifter, the rain ceased, and everything was eerily quiet except for the flow of runoff into the storm drains along the curbsides.

I looked at the picture of Emmy, pinned in-between the glass covering the speedometer and the plastic of my dashboard. It was of her on the back of my dad's pontoon all those years ago, the same night when we made our list. Her green eyes looked even greener with the bay and sunset in the background. In that instant, for the first time since meeting her, not even she could make me smile. I drove to the liquor store down the street from our apartment, made my way home, and moved through the dark, empty hallway to our room. Everything looked like it always had. I cracked open the bottle of whiskey and chugged it until I felt like I was spinning in circles and my head was seconds from exploding. Disoriented, I dropped the bottle, spilling the remaining drink down the front of my already mud-stained suit.

I fell back onto my mattress, practically paralyzed from the ridiculous amount of alcohol flowing through my bloodstream. I laid there, motionless, my eyes struggling to fixate upon the picture of Emmy and I that was sitting on our nightstand. A single tear fell from my eye and hit the pillow resting beneath my head. I closed my eyes, brutally exhausted from the travesty of the day's events. I wasn't going to be able to do this, not without her. I tried my best to fall asleep, but the dizziness and restlessness persisted and insomnia set in. Hours passed before my body could physically take no more. When I rolled over to her side of the bed the following morning, it finally hit me. This was real. This was real.

†

Bone-dry whiskey bottles once covered the carpet of my bedroom, lying motionless as my only beacon of solace after Emma's passing. By that time, nearly one full year had elapsed since her death, and every month had dreadfully crept by. Bills were neglected until I scavenged the money from friends and family who pitied my loss and occasionally sent me checks and gift cards to help me get by. I had dropped my job with J&J, much to the dissatisfaction of my parents and colleagues. My relationship with Ms. Blair and Robbie had nearly dissipated since the end of Emmy's battle, but on the eighth of every month (the day of her passing), I'd always manage to trudge my drunken self down the road to the local flower shop to ship a bouquet to their home, scratching the surface of the bare minimum when it came to my promise of looking after them.

The incessant nagging of my parents amazed me, calling anywhere from three to four times a day to scold me about not reaching back out to J&J and pleading for my job again in a poor attempt at playing the sympathy card. I think back to the time when I had convinced myself that when my minuscule financial resources ran out and all that I was left with was a soul that was battered, bruised, and scarred, and a nonexistent work ethic, that I'd send one last bouquet of flowers to Ms. Blair and Robbie before sitting down in my recliner with a bottle of antidepressants and a fifth of vodka, until I was either in a self-induced coma or had the last remaining pieces of my heart seep out of me and send me six feet under where I'd come to believe I belonged. Regardless of how horrifying it may sound now, I had thought it through from start to finish without any trace of willpower to stop me from ending everything.

I heard this speech one time, about a guy who survived a suicide bombing over in Europe somewhere. He talked about how the area directly around the bomber was the worst, with body parts strewn all over the place and the scene looking like a gruesome war story. The people on the outskirts of the attack were left scarred and burned, but walked away as he did. He said that when someone commits suicide in any other way, the same holds true. Your closest friends and family, those who love you more than anyone or anything, are going to be hurt the most. They're going to be the people who won't have the choice of walking away. So, in the outermost confines of my mind, was Emma. What would she be telling me? To get my act together and grow up? To quit the childish threats of ending my own life, which would ultimately devastate my family beyond repair? Or would she remind me of the promises I made to her, to look after her aunt and brother, to find love again, and to never lose faith in God? Hundreds of thoughts

flushed in and out of my feeble mind every day, as to how I could possibly

live up to any one of those promises. Sure, commitments like these wouldn't

have even crossed my train of thought if they were to anyone else, but since

they were to Em, I knew I would cave in and do exactly what she would

have wanted. Even at the time in my life where everything was hopeless and

meaningless at best, those promises to Emma stood resolutely. Because of

'always.'

Rekindling my faith with this invisible mediocracy in the clouds

known as "God" was perhaps the biggest challenge for me as I desperately

tried to rediscover myself as a person and get back to a life on Earth that was

remotely close to "okay." How could anyone that holy take accountability

for dragging me through such an emotionally draining, utterly miserable, and

frankly psychotic period of my life without any hint of explanation or

justification? Every day was a reversed nightmare—I woke up to horror in

my reality and sought after my world of imagination when I went to sleep.

Instead of being scared in a dream and waking up in relief to the real world,

I'd look to spend as much of my time with my head on the pillow and my body under the layers of sheets, trying to get away from the depression that clouded my actual life. What could "He" possibly have in store for me, and how could I ever believe that there was some plan for my life, now that the person I loved the most was torn from the warmth of my arms? God took away my angel on Earth so that He could have her to Himself in heaven. I couldn't even begin to envision forgiving Him for that. But I at least had to start trying.

It took months for me to convince myself (or fool myself) into believing that any step forward would yield something worthwhile. To put it bluntly, I didn't think I stood a snowball's chance in Hell with any effort at "getting clean" and landing my life back on track. I never considered myself an alcoholic, but the instinctive reach for the bottle was the first obstacle I strived to overcome. Throughout all those months, the intricately shaped glasses that cluttered our once cleanly and organized apartment stood as my only friend and were the only thing that could temporarily erase the agony and worthlessness that poisoned my mind. The willpower I had to quit was stronger than I had initially thought, and every time I felt the need to fall back on the booze for comfort, the image in the back of my mind of Emma scowling at me eventually led to me pouring all the remaining liquid down the sink and hauling an unfathomably heavy recycling bin full of bottles out to the curb. I had forgotten what the carpet in my room had looked like until I finally disposed of all the bottles, wrappers, and napkins. I guess it was a start. Maybe even something to be proud of.

My flabby stomach was surely nothing to take pride in, and I was sure about that much. Since Emma had passed, I was up over twenty-five pounds, and not an ounce of that weight gain was muscle. I hadn't even hinted at working out or going to the gym in months, and not just because I couldn't afford it. I started a minimal workout routine and began eating healthier when I did decide to sit down for a meal. I knew that my finances were dwindling, almost to the point of sheer bankruptcy. Every part of my being dreaded the thought of stepping back out into the workforce, or even the world outside my apartment walls in general. This wasn't just because of my appearance, my strong-willed refusal towards anything involving effort, or even my crappy state of mind. It was no secret that everyone from high school, college, and work had by then started to refer to me as a drunken nutcase or a socially inept mess, so I was justifiably horrified of judgment. Then again, I began to realize that I brought a lot of that on myself. I allowed the remaining half of me to die when Emma did. She would have never expected, nor wanted, that out of me. She saw potential in me that even I was incapable of recognizing, so I needed to make her proud of me once more. But in order to do that, I had to first learn to find pride in myself. As with most things on the road to recovery, that was far easier said than done—I can promise you that.

I scavenged through newspapers and tore through the web, looking for a job that would suit my interests while also leaving me out of the scope of disappointment and cattiness that my neighbors, family, and friends would likely sling in my direction. Every opening dealt with some type of janitorial duty, being stuck in a copy room, or bussing tables at a restaurant. No disrespect to anyone with those occupations, but I had a dual-major degree from one of the best schools in the country, and I wasn't too keen on lowering my professional standards that much quite yet. I couldn't help but feel a little embarrassed towards myself throughout the entire process, looking back at the person I once was and all of the promise my career held. Although it wasn't about the money, I could feel my ego numbing as I looked at jobs typically filled by high school students. I thought about where I may have found myself if I stuck with J&J after all. I could have a higher salary, perhaps a new company car, or even my first ever promotion had I not thrown fire into the wind and turned into a quitter.

I let my life go down the drain, and everyone my age was well into their career or relationship, happier and more successful than ever. And then, almost as if Emma herself had posted it in big, bold lettering, there was a teaching assistant position at Palmer Academy, a school for children with special needs and mental handicaps, right down the road from my apartment complex. After all this time, I'm still baffled at why I felt the need to apply for the position that day. I was a recovering heartbreak who hadn't socialized with anyone or anything for months on end. I didn't have a degree that would deem me a suitable applicant for the position, and I had no clue how to handle children, let alone children with those sorts of disabilities. I had always wanted kids, but that dream, along with hundreds of others, took flight when Emma grew her own wings and flew away.

It was a short time after that when I received a phone call from the academy, asking about my availability to come in for an interview as a follow-up to my online application. At first, I was a bit hesitant, but I eventually agreed and told the receptionist (whose soft-spoken, almost angelic voice I remember to this day) that I'd stop by the following morning. I was so nervous! It was going to be my first interview since college, which felt like an eternity ago in the rearview mirror of my life. My nerves were all shaken up, mostly because at that point I had about half the confidence as what I did when I was at UMD, which wasn't even a lot to begin with.

When I first walked into the main entrance, I was taken back by the bright colors that coated every wall around me, most of which came from finger paintings that appeared to be drawn by the students and low-hanging string lights that laced the ceiling edges. I was greeted with a warm "hello" by the woman behind the front desk, whose voice sounded perfectly in tune with who called me on the phone only a day prior. She limply led the way as I followed her down the corridor, passing nearly a dozen classrooms filled with special needs children of all ages, working on crafts, dancing to music, and watching intently as their respective instructors flipped through page after page of picture books, much to the delight of the attentive pupils. It was precious, really. I knew how much I valued that time as a child, sitting and listening to every word my teacher spoke. I didn't know if I could even call myself that, a "teacher," if I were to get the job. Whether I'd act as an assistant or even a secretary to someone, I honestly had no idea whatsoever.

The soft-spoken old woman rounded the corner and stepped into an office area, which couldn't have been much larger than a storage closet. It was so confined that I could feel her breath with every word she spoke. I sat down with a less-than-enthusiastic smile on my face, prepping myself for every possible question that was bound to be thrown my way. It soon became apparent that this wasn't going to be like any of the serious business interviews that I'd had in the past. Not to question her authority or her experience with interviews, but I couldn't see someone so light and happy-looking grilling me with professional, in-depth questions. Her dark brown eyes were so… welcoming? Reassuring, maybe? She must've sat there smiling at me for the first whole minute. For some reason, it wasn't as awkward as it sounds.

She looked at me almost as if she was ready to reach out and hug me at any given second. "I know who you are, Liam." I was taken aback, then doubting that she simply knew about me based off of my application. "Yes, ma'am, that's my name, please don't wear it out!" My pitiful attempt at breaking the ice and starting off the interview on a light note never seemed to phase her and reluctantly led to me blushing in sheer embarrassment. "I know why you're here, sweetheart. I know about your loss, about all of the pain and fear that you've been dealing with. I want you to know that from the bottom of my heart, I'm not only astonished, but also proud to see you trying to recapture your life again." Still unaware and borderline freaked out as to who this woman was or how she knew about my scenario, I instinctively darted my eyes towards the floor and nervously began twiddling my thumbs, as if to comfort myself and divert my mind away from the thought of Emma. Now was not the right time. Here was not the right place.

I was on the edge of my seat, sweating bullets as to what her next comment or question would be, fearing that I'd have to elaborate to this random lady about my history with alcoholism and being a social hermit, all so she could dictate whether I could be trusted with those elementary aged kids. Fantastic. She read me like a book and immediately answered the question that she could tell was puzzling me. "My son, Melvin, and I live down the hall from you. I think he even looked after your wife on the evening you went out ring shopping for her, some time ago." I looked back up into her eyes, only to see a gentle tear trickle down her puffy, red cheek, and inaudibly fall onto her lap. "He's been worried about you, Liam. He's only seen you twice over the past however many months and is always hesitant about knocking to check up on you. He saw the bottles of liquor in your recycling bin the other day and called me at work, completely in disbelief as to how you could still be alive." I was at a loss for words, half of me feeling selfish and the other half feeling shy about the entire scenario.

"I'm going to give you this job, son. I know you didn't come in expecting this, but I made up my mind that if you showed up to give us a chance—to give yourself a chance—then I would do all in my power to return the favor. I know the pay that was advertised wasn't too substantial, and I've already talked to the board about taking a small pay-cut so that you can earn a little more to help get yourself back up on your feet. The value you're going to find in this job will be greater than any paycheck, and you need a big heart to work with these kids, but I know you have just that. You're going to change their lives, and if you're willing enough, maybe you'll let them change yours too."

I'd forgotten what it was like to feel so strongly about anyone, anything, or any situation like the one I found myself in just then. "Thank you" could do no justice as to how I felt in that moment. I slowly stood up, extended my arms, and hugged her with all the might that I had in my body. My eyes welled up, but I refused to cry. That was the first day in a very long time that I saw the spirit of Emma in someone else. The fact that she was willing to lend a helping hand to me going strictly off of my story was unheard of. In all my times talking to Melvin, never would I have guessed that he'd care enough about me to express worry to his mom, who somehow managed to elude me as a neighbor up until that point. It took a while for me to see it, but there was still some genuine goodness in the cracked void known as my life.

I began work that following Monday, and my nerves were wreaking havoc on the inner walls of my mind. What was I supposed to expect? Was my outfit of a collared shirt with a tie and khakis too formal, or perhaps too informal? Per my instructions, I arrived promptly at eight o'clock in the morning and navigated my way towards Room 22, where I was set to meet with Mrs. Belanger, who was responsible for the day-to-day activities of the children who were supposed to be between the ages of six and ten. She offered up some brief chit-chat as to what all I'd be assigned to do: read to the class, supervise recess, and clean up their classroom at the day's end, in addition to some miscellaneous duties that would vary on a daily basis. I had no doubt that I could master snacks and reading, but I knew that arts and crafts wouldn't be my forte!

When the students came pouring into the classroom after being dropped off by their special school vans (you know, the yellow ones with "school students" stickered across the back hatch), they slowed their frenzied pace and looked at me with a "who the heck are you" expression smeared across almost every face. I still chuckle about that, trying to put myself in their shoes as some strange man shows up one day out of the blue and throws a wrench into their daily routine. I politely introduced myself as Liam. I wasn't much of a last name kind of guy, and I figured being referred to by my first name would make them feel a little more comfortable, almost as if I were a student just like the rest of them. I told them that I'd be helping Mrs. Belanger out in class for the foreseeable future and how excited I was to become their friend. They shyly nodded and continued towards their desks, leaving me wondering if that was a good sign, or if I was already down in the count.

I sat patiently in the back of the room as the special needs kids worked diligently on some simple math problems, made two or three crafts, and enjoyed a pre-lunch snack of pretzels and animal crackers. When I was given the cue to kick off story time prior to lunch and recess, all twenty of them eagerly circled up on the shaggy, red carpet that covered the back half of the room, acting like they'd done it a million times or like I was a drill instructor and they were newbies to the corps. Before I began reading "The Very Hungry Caterpillar," I took a moment to scan over the crowd in front of me, taking it all in for the first time. Some of the youngsters were more noticeably affected by their disorders than others, but all of them were adorable beyond what words could express. I couldn't help but chuckle when I saw the little guy in the back whose glasses had a ridiculously bent frame scoot an inch or two closer to the precious little blond-haired girl with Downs Syndrome directly to his left. I complimented little Scott, the only kid whose name I remembered from our brief introductions, sitting front and center, on his Orioles shirt. His toothless smile was enough to send me laughing, reclining back in the squeaky rocking chair. Despite not knowing why I was laughing, a few students began to giggle too.

I was warming up to the atmosphere far quicker than I could have possibly imagined, and to call it a breath of fresh air would have been an understatement. All throughout the story, the kids squealed and giggled, and they all broke into roaring applause when the final page was flipped and the book was closed. Mrs. B stood in the doorway, looking proud of how smoothly this transition was turning out to be. Was it really because of me, or were those kids just that excited for story time that they'd react that way for just about anyone? As I followed up the rear of the single file line, I took notice to the fact that, much like Emma, these children, despite the horrible card that life had dealt them, refused to look at the simplest of pleasures in life with anything less than a smile on their face and a pounding heart in their chests. There was beauty in their hardship. I dropped my head, closing my eyes and realizing that all of this wasn't a coincidence. I needed to stop overthinking the fact that there were hundreds of overlooked blessings in my life and things that I took for granted each day, which simply wasn't the case with these kids. There was, indeed, a higher power behind this comeback of mine, whether I was man enough to admit it yet or not. Without thinking even farther into it, I sprinted down the hall so as to not be the last one out the door to the playground.

✝

Weeks came and went, every passing day being just as much fun as the day prior. I started to lose sight of the fact that I was being paid to do this "job." It was as though I was beginning to feel like a kid again, and despite my heart growing cold and lonely after Emma's passing, nothing would ever inhibit me from losing my inner child—that much was evident. I think that's part of the reason why Emma and I were so close and "clicked" from square one. We never shied away from acting like kids around each other, whether it was at home by ourselves or out in public doing childish antics to cross them off of our bucket list. In reality, those kids were probably a heck of a lot more mature than I was in a lot of respects. I grew closer with all of the kids, memorizing not only their names, but their favorite colors, activities, books, and snacks. It made me feel like I was actually good at something, without having to work very hard at it—a feeling that was a rarity to me. I dwelled on what it must have been like to be a father, the strongest pillar in someone's life from the inception of their birth until the day you lay silent, six feet under the white dogwood leaves. A father, someone whose life revolves around his children and their safety, their success, their trust, their hope, and their happiness. I felt like a father to those students, in my own little regard. I liked to convince myself that I had their trust, that I strengthened their sense of hope, and that I sent them home with fun stories to tell their families before crawling into bed at night. But then again, maybe they forgot about me when they walked out of Room 22 at the end of each day, only to remember me as the guy who gave them snacks when they stepped off the bus that next morning. I never really had a way of knowing.

   During that stretch of time, I was spending my evenings repainting the insides of the apartment, posting old collectibles of mine for sale online to earn some extra cash, and reading old works from Poe, Dickinson, and Emerson—something I hadn't done since Emma had passed, which I had missed dearly. Reading and writing proved to be instrumental in getting my life back on track, consuming me with the eloquence of words that calmed me and inspired me simultaneously. I became obsessed with keeping myself healthy and in shape, occasionally remembering to even say a prayer (although they were more obligatory than genuine) before my head hit the pillow at night. My mental health was improving drastically, almost as much as my physical health, but when I did say one of those prayers, it was always the same thing each time. I'd mumble something about looking over my family and our soldiers overseas, ask Him to forgive me for my sins and say "thank you" for his blessings, even when I couldn't quite put my finger on all that many. I was desperately trying to save up my money and turn my life around on its axis. I spent a lot of time exploring the possibility of moving into a smaller home and escaping the miserable haze that loomed over me every time I got into the bed I had always shared with Emma and every time I stepped foot into the shower where we used to draw cute little messages on the steamed glass door before class and work every morning. I needed to get the apartment as spiffy as possible before showing the landlord and asking him to try and get it back out on the market, so in due time, I could pack my bags and head elsewhere.

I ended up with a drawer exclusively for my dirty paint clothes, working tirelessly at patching up the little holes and scratches on the walls that appeared during my months of loneliness and disregard, doing my best to cover all of my bases before the final apartment inspection. My dad used to tell me stories about my grandpa and how he was a painter. It was kind of neat to see things come full circle, although I knew I'd never live up to the work of my Pap. I was still sending flowers to Ms. Blair's home on the eighth of each month and making efforts to talk to her at least twice a week, checking in to see if there was anything she and Robbie needed around the house and to check up on how his baseball season was treating him, amongst other things. It was nice to hear a little bit of liveliness come back into their voices as time went on. I think they too understood that Emma would want for them to move on with their lives, loving each other even stronger than they had when she was still here. I was also rebuilding the connection with my parents and my younger brother, Ken (a freshman soccer player at Towson), which had progressively gotten better as I started putting one foot in front of the other again. I remember feeling their pride and respect, which I hadn't felt since Emma had passed away and I entered into "the dark phase," as I used to call it.

Our list had collected dust, sitting on her nightstand, with the last check being placed beside the "learn Swahili" bullet point. I glanced over at it often, taking note as to how beautiful her handwriting was, almost entirely reflective of her physique and personality, too. I longed to reach over and flip through the milestones yet to be achieved, but the fear of reminiscing and engulfing myself in depression managed to make me withdraw my hand every single time. I finally tidied up the apartment to the point where a bunch of rock star-looking dudes pulled the trigger on splitting the price between the four of them, sending me out the door with a truckload of cardboard boxes that would eventually be unpacked into my new home on Shryock Lane, only a fifteen-minute drive away from Palmer Academy. I grieved for Melvin, as I was confident that my old living space would be turned into a studio with absurdly loud tunes blaring until the latest hours of the night. I finally had a yard to mow and some landscaping projects to occupy myself with, so I was as content as I probably could have been. The yard may have only been as big as an oversized rug, but nonetheless, it was a yard. The home was just barely out of my price range, but with the extra money from selling some old baseball cards online and working odd lawn work jobs on the weekends, I was reasonably certain that I would make it out okay.

The house was in decent shape, with the crimson red shutters nicely complimenting the dark wooden and stained wrap-around porch out front. I envisioned myself on a lovely, white rocking chair during the mornings of summer, watching the dew from the grass slowly disappear with the rising sun, all the while reading some more poems by Dickinson and sipping on a cup of hot tea; pretending to be sophisticated was actually pretty fun to do from time to time. When I saw myself in that tiny home with two bedrooms,

I saw an all-new beginning at chasing a life of newly defined purpose. Maybe I could become friends with the neighbors, or even invite my family, Ms. Blair, and Robbie over for cookouts on the weekends. Perhaps I could mow some cool designs into the front and back yards, just for the fun of it. Who knew where God was supposedly "leading me" with all of it? All I could focus on was making my best friend up in the heavens proud of my efforts and even more proud of who I was trying to become as a young man. I learned how beautiful of a creature pride is and how just a little bit of it can help carry anyone through even the hardest of times. The same goes with strength; yeah, it's all relatively cliché, but when people say "you never realize how strong you are until being strong is the only option you have left," they aren't lying.

There are certain times in our lives where the unimaginable finagles its way into becoming reality, giving us a front-row look at what defying the odds looks like. It was around that time in my life where things had finally managed to plateau and get back to being as "normal" as possible, despite all of the circumstances that had transpired over the past year or so. As far as I can remember, it was a rambunctious Friday afternoon before Easter break, and all of my kids were wound up and ready for the egg hunting festivities, the candy, and the warm weather that the next week was forecasted to entail. Don't get me wrong—if I had the chance to join them, I would go in a heartbeat. I was busy cleaning up their desks, the mess all across the floor, and the remnants of paper that littered the carpet in the back of the room as they pushed and shoved their way out the door and down the hall to the entrance where the buses were lined up to take them home. Although I loved these kids to pieces, it was a chore having to clean up after them every single day, always feeling amazed by what I happened to find in the crevasses all around the classroom. Mrs. Belanger had already been out of town since Wednesday of that week for a short trip to the shore with her girlfriends before having to spend the remainder of the holiday concocting meals in the kitchen and catching up on household chores that had been neglected for quite some time. I thought that those kinds of excursions were only suited for younger ladies, but I guess she refused to let her age get the best of her. Easily put, I was the head-honcho for a whopping three days—lucky me!

When I had satisfyingly swept the last pile of litter into the dustpan and poured it into the trash, I casually grabbed my keys and jacket and made my way to the door. I was always the last one to leave the school each day, long after all of the students had boarded the buses and the staff had fled home to the comfort of their families' love. Yes, a lot of it had to do with my OCD in keeping the room orderly, but that was beside the point. Making my way out to the parking lot, I took notice through the window that there was a petite woman standing by my truck, with her oversized pea coat wrapped tightly over her shoulders, covering just enough of her face that it made identifying her from that far away a nearly impossible feat. Puzzled at who it was, I took my time locking the front entrance doors and double-checking that everything was left in the proper place for our return at the conclusion of the holiday break. Nearing my truck, it was made clear to me that the woman standing there was, in fact, Melvin's mom, the school's receptionist. She had been patiently watching me for the past five minutes or so and looked relieved when I eventually made it over to where she was standing. Still humbled by her generosity in giving me the teaching opportunity, I instinctively bent down, gave her a hug, and thanked her again for treating me as if I was her own son in my attempt at writing a comeback story. Her warm smile was enough to take my attention away from the frigid breeze that was nipping at my extremities.

"Would you like to join me and Melvin at this Sunday's church service?" she asked. Hesitant, knowing that I hadn't been to a formal service since Emma was healthy, I opened my mouth to decline politely, but the look on her face left me with the impression that she wasn't going to accept "no thank you, ma'am" as an answer. I coughed to avoid an awkward lapse before answering and reluctantly nodded my head, much to her delight. The smile on her face spanned from ear to ear, with her expression soon turning to one of frustration as she began rummaging through her purse until she had located a little communion card with the words "St. Christopher's Lutheran Church" printed in deep purple lettering across the top and an address found just below it. "I'll see you there at nine o'clock, sharp! We usually sit in the back pew, but try and dress nicely anyway. After all, it is Easter Sunday." She parted with another tight hug, and scurried across the pavement to her old Ford Taurus across the lot while I stood in silence, loosely gripping the communion card in my right hand.

Although it was a few days away, my nerves were already running rampant. I had only been back in the loop with the whole prayer thing for a few months, and I still wasn't entirely convinced that God truly existed or that He was a "good guy." I still had no explanation for why He'd take away someone as perfect as Emma. No matter how many times I tried to wrap my mind around it, I couldn't. I crawled into the front seat of my truck, turned on the heat, and pulled out the letter from Emma that I always kept in my wallet. I must have read it no less than five times before putting the shifter into drive and making my way home as the sun sloped gently down below the crests of the surrounding hills and out of sight. The Big Dipper looked a lot brighter than usual that night. Emma always said she thought it looked like a dog; I still have a hard time seeing how.

It wasn't ironic that Easter Sunday was dreary; a handful of overcast clouds presented us with a grayish haze, which dampened the festive attitude of almost everyone. I had trouble falling asleep the night before because of the whirl of emotions clogging every pore of my mind, thinking about stepping foot into a church again. I wasn't sure why I was struggling with this so much. After all, I'd always been a devout Christian growing up and had been open with my faith, all the way up until Emma passed away and the whole concept of a higher being became much more difficult for me to accept than ever before. I made a promise to Emma that I wouldn't lose my relationship with and my faith in God, so I was trying my best to fulfill it. I had, admittedly, gotten better at focusing more on the blessings in my life than the dispositions it carried. Sometimes I felt like He actually had my back, but the haunting reality of the past few years always managed to conquer what little faith I had momentarily dug up.

Stepping outside that morning, the warm mud squished beneath my leather dress shoes and stained the lower cuff of my khakis as I made my way from the porch, across the front yard, and towards my truck parked along the edge of the street. In all honesty, I'm surprised I even made it to St. Christopher's that morning because navigating the GPS on my phone in one hand and maneuvering the steering wheel with the other nearly proved disastrous. Needless to mention, the fact that my shoes were already muddy led me to assume that the day was going to suck.

I arrived shortly before the service began, shaking the hands of unfamiliar faces, faking a smile, and trying my best to avoid as much eye contact as possible in case anyone was to recognize me. I scooched and folded my skinny figure through the masses of people until I could slide into the last pew on the right, finding Melvin and his mother looking joyous (and slightly surprised) at my prompt arrival. After some small talk, the vast majority of which dealt with their new and obnoxiously loud neighbors— yes, I called it—a short and chubby pastor emerged from the pulpit with the glistening white Alb cloaked over her shoulders. Without being able to draw on the offering card as I did as a kid, I had to listen to every church announcement from some soup kitchen event to St. Christopher's big mission trip to Honduras that upcoming summer. Their hope was to build a brand-new orphanage for a bunch of children who were displaced by a horrific fire at their last orphanage location. The congregation's thundering applause after the announcement was enough to make my ears ring and brought everyone in the sanctuary to their feet.

The service began with the congregation singing an array of hymns. I mouthed all of them (because quite frankly, I couldn't sing to save my life), followed by the reading of some biblical verses before children's time. The pastor handed out Goldfish crackers to the youngsters and talked about how they should fish for a life that God would be proud of: minding their manners, trying their very best in school, and always being on their best behavior. It made me miss my class, even though it was only a couple of days since I last saw them. The pastor stood up after dispersing the kids back into the crowd and proceeded to voice her sermon about love and its power in the purest of forms. Quoting 1 Corinthians 13: 4-8, she proudly rehearsed that "Love is patient and kind. Love does not envy, nor boast; it is neither arrogant nor rude. It does not insist on its own way; it is not irritable, and it is not resentful. Love does not rejoice at wrongdoing, but rejoices with the truth. Love bears all things, believes all things, hopes all things, and endures all things."

I couldn't believe the testimonial that flooded my ears, because throughout the entire process of losing my best friend, there was one remaining stitch to the patchwork called faith, and it was this very verse. I remember Emma quoting this a time or two, indirectly. Whenever she mentioned it, I always thought that it sounded even more beautiful because it came from her lips. I may have doubted in God. I may have questioned myself. But love? Love was forever. Love was always, and deep down inside my heart, I knew that. There was never a moment in my few, precious years with Emma that I questioned the purity and the enormity of the blessing that we labeled as "love." It was passionate, and it was humorous. It was an obstacle at times, but love was always a fight worth having and a light that needed to be emitted. Sitting in the back pew that squeaked and squawked with every slight movement on that Easter Sunday, I again began to believe. I realized that in the time since Emma had joined the rest of God's angels, I had learned more about myself and life, more about what actually matters and what's worth fighting for, than I ever have. It was almost as though I was more consumed by euphoria without her there than what I was with her there, and I accepted that it was now a battle only I was able to fight. God had more in store for this journey towards rekindling my happiness, but patience was ultimately the virtue I needed above all else.

By the time I refocused myself on the service, it was almost over. I slid a few bucks into the offering bowl as it weaved its way in and out of each pew, only for the pastor to raise it up at the altar and give thanks as they did at my church when I was younger. I followed Melvin's lead (which was annoyingly slow) through the communion procession, up to the front of the chapel and back around the side of the pews. The pinch of bread that I was handed could have probably fed a third-world country, and the wine was lip-puckering sweet. Minutes later, the service had reached its end, and the congregation flooded through the exit doors, long awaiting the festivities with their families that the remainder of the day was set to bring.

Melvin's mother was oddly persistent in introducing me to the pastor on our way out, which struck me with a tad bit of concern. Did this woman really think I needed this much of a Christian dosage in my life? I felt like I

was destined to go to Hell a few months ago, but she, more so than anyone,

should have noticed that I had finally gotten my act together and was doing

all I could to avoid the fiery depths of purgatory down below. I would have

loved to bust out an excuse about being busy with another commitment, but

she pretty much knew that I didn't have anyone or anything to tie me down

that day. I mean, this was my first public appearance in forever and a half, so

talking to a pastor probably couldn't hurt. We patiently waited for everyone

else to leave the sanctuary before walking to the front of the church to the

pudgy preacher who was having a comically difficult time with removing

her Alb. Just as I was about to offer to help her out, she emerged from the

inside-out mess with her face left red and flustered. Melvin's mother

introduced me as their "family friend," and the pastor's expression

immediately turned to one of sympathy, almost as if to say "Oh, you must be

the guy whose wife died." Yeah, awkward was the perfect way of describing

it.

  "You must be Liam. I've heard a lot of great things about you. I just

want you to know that our Lord, Jesus Christ, is proud of you and what

you're doing for the special needs kids in our community. And above all else, what you're doing for yourself. I'm sure Emma—that's her name, right?" I slowly nodded. "Yes, I'm sure that she's looking down on you right now with a tear in her eye and a lot of pride in her heart. I know you're still in a lot of pain, but there's a reason for all of this, even if you haven't quite figured it out yet. God's love is greater than our disappointments and His plans for our lives are greater than our dreams, dear. Whatever you must do to discover the real you, don't be daunted if the rest of the world looks on in shock." By that point, her hand was on my shoulder, her arm fully extended to reach up that high, looking deep into my wandering eyes. I whispered "Thank you," and gently put my hand on hers, trying to subtly get it to move away.

"Now, speaking of reasons, there's a reason you were brought here this morning, aside from getting you back into the realm of worship." She walked over to the nearest pew and motioned for me, Melvin, and his mother to come and sit down with her. Unsure of where this was going, I looked for some reassurance from Melvin and his mom, and sure enough, they both looked back at me with their lips curved upward in the softest of grins. It was creepy, honestly, but I tried my best to just go with it and not think too much into things. "It's my understanding that you're quite talented when it

comes to speaking Spanish and understanding the language, is that correct?"
My stomach started to churn because I knew almost immediately where this
was going. "Yes, ma'am, I'd like to think I'm fairly good at speaking and
understanding it. I studied in the Dominican and majored in it when I went
to UMD a few years back." Melvin and his mom had, by then, started
whispering to one another, just quiet enough to escape the range of my
listening ears. "Well, I'm sure you heard my announcement earlier about our
upcoming mission trip to Honduras this July. The church council and I have
shared some concern as to the communication factor in dealing with the
locals and the church we'll be partnering with down there. The priest's
English is poor at best, and to make things run as smoothly as possible, we'd
need a translator to aid us in bringing both sides of the operation together. I
heard you've recently moved into a new house just outside of town and are
settling into a big financial commitment, so I know this is a lot to ask of
you."

She slowly moved her hand off of my shoulder (I never even realized
that she put it back there once we all sat down) and proceeded to take my
right hand into hers. "But, after pulling some strings and reconfiguring some
allocations of the church's budget, we have the money set aside to cover

your travel, food, and lodging expenses for the week. I know this is all hitting you at once, but having someone like you find their way through the doors of our sanctuary is the answer to our biggest prayer. Seriously, Liam, we've been asking God to shed some light on this dilemma—you, son, are that light." Bewildered at the fact that this woman I had just met was offering me an all-expenses paid vacation and claiming that I was some sort of "godsend," my mouth dried up, and I was legitimately at a loss for words. "And, if you want to know the other way I see it, son, I really do trust the fact that this is a chance for you to get back on track with your faith. I could see it clear as day during service that you were on pins and needles. I understand where it's stemming from and I know it's easy to blame Him, but you'll be amazed by His work in due time."

I knew that my schedule would permit me to go on this excursion because school would be let out for summer by that point in time, and I'd be stuck at home all by my lonesome for three months, working on little projects around the house and catching up on some reading and writing I was planning on doing. I could sense how badly she wanted me to say "yes" just by the shear plea in her voice and her eyes that resembled those of a puppy. Standing there in that colossal doorway of St. Christopher's, seconds felt like hours as I weighed the situation at hand. To most anyone, it would be a no-brainer, but I was still getting my life and my faith back on track, and I was unsure if it was too big of a step for me to take—and one that was too soon at that. I could hear Emma in the back of my head, shouting for me to accept the generous offer and to make the most of it, because of life being too short for regrets. If anyone knew that, it was her.

Fading back into the moment, I did something completely un-Liam like and flat out said, "Absolutely. Count me in." Neither Melvin, his mother, nor the pastor was as astonished at the words that escaped my mouth as much as I was. For once, I didn't let my brain fog the process of something in my heart. I didn't hesitate for long. I didn't let fear or uncertainty dictate a decision. I took a risk with the hopes of rising to the occasion. It was satisfying, taking a leap of faith. As far as I was concerned, the pros outweighed the cons by a long shot. Pastor McWilliams immediately reached up and gave me the biggest, most unexpected kiss on the forehead and began to say a prayer of thanks for my willingness to help and my bravery in embarking on this journey to salvage my faith. "Dear God, I know that this answer is by no means an easy one for Liam, but please continue to instill reassurance in him that he made the right choice this Easter morning. The lives that he's already touched are but a mere fraction of what he's going to accomplish and who he's going to aid during this mission trip and over the remainder of his life. You've created something extraordinary with this boy. I know he doesn't yet understand your reasoning and your intentions for the rest of his days, but please work to show him that, despite his doubts, the best days of his life are yet to be had. In the name of the Father, of the Son, and of the Holy Spirit, Amen."

After leaving her with my contact information in order to touch base up until the trip, I exerted all of my force into getting the old, wooden front door of St. Christopher's pried open. When it finally swung free from its rusted hinges, I emerged along the street, the sun shining through the clouds, engulfing everything in sight with a cloak of light. I smiled, walking across the street to my truck. The memory of me prying open the Weaver Hill Cemetery gate and making my way over to my truck in the rain flashed across my mind. While it was pouring then, the sun was now out and shining brightly. I stepped up and into my seat, glancing down at the picture of Emmy on my dashboard before pulling up to the stop sign and popping a right-hand turn to navigate towards my parent's place. I was excited to see them and show them how much I've changed since they last saw me. It was exciting to not be alone again on a holiday as big as Easter. And from the bottom of my heart, I was already feeling a little excited about that mission trip, too. None of it was coincidental. This was something bigger—much, much bigger.

Whether it may sound cliché or not, the next two months flew by. Days didn't trudge on like they once had at the beginning of my time working at the academy, which I was unbelievably grateful for. I'd already taught my kids—it's weird saying "my kids," isn't it?—the basics of addition, subtraction, multiplication, and division, and they fell in love with it almost immediately. You would never have been able to grasp just how quickly they picked up on the concepts and mastered the work. The end of the school year was so bittersweet because I was starting to get excited at the progress of the class, and I longed for nothing more than to take their reading and math skills to the next level. Mrs. Belanger could see the rapid succession with their homework assignments, and would even share with me emails sent in by some of the parents, praising the strides we helped their sons and daughters make throughout that academic year.

On the last day of school, I made sure to give every student a huge hug and a chance to pull from a ten-pound bag of miscellaneous candies I bought from the store—$5.99, talk about a steal. Most of them just gave me a weak one-armed hug that I could barely feel around my hip, yelling, "See you next year, Liam!" as they bolted out the door and down the hall towards the entrance of the building where all of the vans were lined up for what would be the last time in months. Next year was still up in the air for me. I was uncertain of what opportunities would come my way and what role finances would play in my decision to stay at the academy or search for a higher paying job elsewhere. Regardless of what I would end up doing or what path I would take, my heart would never allow me just to walk away from these kids altogether. Even if I had to come back and volunteer on the rare occasion, it would be the absolute least I could do, seeing as though they had given me the chance at getting my life in order and making me feel good on the inside again.

I was tidying things up in the room as Mrs. B gathered her belongings and wished me a blessed and safe summer before scurrying out of the school almost as fast as the kids. I made sure to erase the chalkboard, wipe down the windows and mop the floor, vacuum the rug in the back of the room, and wrap it all up by spritzing down the desks with disinfectant spray. Oh, and making sure that the underneath compartment where they'd often store their pens, extra snacks, and craft supplies was clean. As I made my way to the final row of desks, the garbage can that I was dragging behind me was almost filled to the brim with empty glue sticks, crumbs, forgotten milk cartons, dried out markers, broken pencils, paper remnants, you name it! With three desks left to clean out, I casually reached my hand into the undercarriage of the desk like I did with every one prior, cringing at what might be lurking in the confines of the unseen territory within. Surprisingly enough, all I managed to come across was a tiny, sealed envelope addressed to "Mr. Liam." Perplexed, I walked to the front of the class to get my bearings straight and to put into perspective who sat where throughout the course of the year. It dawned on me that the desk belonged to a little blond-haired, blue-eyed girl named Amber who sat in the back of the class.

She was always the last one to go out to recess, the last one to finish her crafts and snacks, and would always offer up her seat or place in line for her friends. I could tell that, despite being a petite little girl with pink glasses, her heart was as big as that of an adult. I couldn't even begin to imagine what that letter held inside, but I carefully tore open the edges and slid out a lined sheet of paper that was folded neatly in half, taking notice of the see-through, marker-written words awaiting my curious eyes on the other side. I turned over the sheet and sat down in her chair, my bent knees almost taller than the desk itself.

Mr. Liam,

Thanks you fore helping me on my homwork and crafs and snaks this yeer. I had a loot of fun an lyked wen you red to us. Im hapy you came heer. You are my freind. I hop I am yurs to.

Luve,

Amber

Misspellings and illegible words aside, I was used to reading my students' work and found it pretty easy to decipher. I had no clue when she wrote this, whether she left it there on purpose, or if she just forgot it before leaving earlier that afternoon. Saying that my heart was warmed by that letter wouldn't even be close to summarizing how I genuinely felt on the inside. I had a hard time accepting that she actually took the time to sit down and write a personal note to me, out of all people, thanking me for my efforts in the classroom and for being a friend to her. I pulled out my wallet, took out the note from Emma, and began to read that, too. I couldn't help but find a sense of pride in myself. I'd managed to connect with those children on a level much deeper than just student and teacher. To them (Amber in particular), I was looked at as a friend—a friend! I'd be lying if I said I didn't consider her to be mine, too. I folded up her note and tucked it into my wallet right next to Emma's, finished cleaning the last couple of desks, and locked the door before strolling down the empty hall, flinging open the front door, and getting in my truck to drive home and enjoy my first real evening of summer vacation.

Sitting with my feet kicked up on my cheap coffee table, watching the Orioles game, I reread both letters out loud, falling more in love with each one with every line I read. I awoke around 3 a.m. to find both pieces of paper lying on my lap and the TV still on, the rerun of the game just about over. I stumbled back to my bedroom and wiggled my way in-between the sheets. Though it felt like what took an eternity, I finally got to feel how nice it was to sleep comfortably again.

In the two-month time frame between the end of school and the trip to Honduras, I made a genuine effort to keep myself busy, healthy, and continuously working to build up my bank account. Tedious projects around the house like painting, landscaping, and miscellaneous renovations consumed almost every hour of every day. It deserved to feel more like a home instead of just a house. I was doing some janitorial work at night for the school, just to put some more money away for the house remodeling budget, car insurance, and other bills. Each Friday night, I'd drive to St. Christopher's to meet with the mission group and cover the finer details of the trip, to see what exactly I'd have to expect regarding the translation aspect of things, and to learn more about the projects I'd be assigned to work on while with the group.

According to Pastor McWilliams, our efforts would be concentrated on helping to build a new orphanage, as the one in La Colonia (near Roatan) had recently collapsed after a pretty severe electrical problem led to an unexpected blaze. The building had caught fire and practically sent the place up in flames with the kids still sleeping inside. Supposedly, one of the guys in our group was an electrician, which I assumed wasn't merely a coincidence. They usually had pizza delivered to the church for all of us and did a fairly good job of giving us a chance to get to know one another before our big trip. I was one of about twenty guys, all of whom looked as though they were anywhere between thirty and fifty years old. We also had a fair share of women coming along, which seemed to balance things out pretty nicely. I grew close with Pastor McWilliams over the few months of meeting about our journey below the equator. The first thing out of her mouth every time she saw me was always, "How are things coming along with the house?" with a subtle hint of wanting to come and see it. She'd talk about her twin daughters and how things were treating them with ballet, before gossiping about her husband and his reluctance to do anything but sit around and play Xbox all the time, which I found to be hilarious given his wife's profession. Despite her title as a pastor, she was a pretty down-to-Earth lady, although I would have never originally guessed it. Talking to her more regularly made me feel at ease with my decision and my confidence in the expedition awaiting us.

By the time our trip rolled around in July, I'd already lost about twenty pounds from my workout routine, had a decent tan from working outside, and had finally finished a lot of miscellaneous projects around the house. All of that in addition to maintaining my sobriety for almost a year, I couldn't have been in a better frame of mind about myself both physically and mentally. Sitting by the window after boarding our flight, I couldn't help but feel heartache. I wished more than anything that Emma were there to hold my hand as the plane was taking off, thrusting us back into our seats. I wished she were there to pick and nag over who would get the window seat on the way home, too. I thought about our list and how flying to Greece was the biggest dream that we shared together. But we were never going to do any of those things. That list was a mere scrap piece of paper tucked into some nightstand drawer of mine, collecting dust with its ink fading away.

The flight out of BWI shot us out to Salt Lake City for a short layover before hauling us the whole way down to Juan Manuel Gálvez International Airport, where we frantically sought after our baggage in the claims area for almost a full hour. Exhausted from air time and all of our energy depleted, the thirty of us crammed into a bus that I tracked down— not trying to brag—that drove us to La Colonia. After settling into our hotel rooms around three o'clock in the morning on that Sunday, we all decided to rest up for a few hours before congregating in the hotel lobby to map out the day's activities. The first step was for me to explain to them some of the basic words, phrases, and expressions that they were bound to see and hear throughout their work week. I knew I would likely be the busiest out of everyone, bouncing from native worker to native worker, relaying directions and commands to the rest of our team. That same morning, we arrived on scene to see one giant concrete slab surrounded by about fifteen workers wearing ripped up jeans and t-shirts drenched in sweat, making it apparent that they'd already been working hard for several hours before we arrived.

As we approached, a few toothless smiles snuck out from underneath their facial hair as they waved and motioned us over to the nearby mobile trailer. The head of construction introduced himself as Luis and began outlining the duties of our group, which I had to translate into English for them. He was a tall, lean-looking fellow who couldn't have been older than thirty or forty years old. Following his lead, the rest of the volunteers and I began hoisting up the long planks of wood, which served to be the frame and base of support for the building. It was helpful that the men we brought along were strong and could lift just as much, if not more, than the seemingly older, more experienced workers there. A little after noontime, the priest from the local church paid us a visit, and his English was just as difficult to understand as what Pastor McWilliams had once alluded to. I conversed with him in Spanish, which seemed to ease his anxiousness over speaking with us foreigners. I always appreciated how humble the Latinos felt when someone from another walk of life could speak their tongue.

He went on to explain that the fifty-plus orphans, who were displaced after the fire, had been housed in the old, derelict school building down the road. Locals had resorted to donating food to help feed the children, who were left to sleep on bug-infested rugs and dirty blankets. I could tell how much the community cared for those children, and although their living conditions were far from ideal, it was all that their neighbors could muster for the time being because all remaining funds (which were minuscule to begin with) were poured into purchasing materials for the new construction project. Hearing the heartbreak that plagued the high-spirited townspeople made me and the rest of my group want to work even harder towards getting this place up and running before our plane left the runway in less than a week. We worked hard for another six or seven hours, late into that first evening. Our arms were left scalded by the sun, covered in sweat, riddled with bug bites, and crusted over with mud and dirt.

As the sun quickly sank out of sight beyond the line of trees on the outskirts of the town's edge, we gathered our belongings and trudged exhaustedly back to the hotel. I remember savoring every one of the frigid water droplets as they shot out of the cracked shower nozzle, soaking my hair, then eventually the rest of my body. It took every ounce of strength not to lay down in that shower basin, but instead, I just leaned my forehead against the shower wall and smiled, with thoughts of the orphaned children giggling and running around aimlessly in their new home racing through my mind. After stepping out of the shower, which by then had a dark ring of dirt circling around the drain, I dried off with a towel and slumped myself into bed, butt-naked and far too tired to even put on a pair of boxer briefs. As I laid in the bed of that hotel, Emma was again all that I could focus on. Why couldn't she be there, helping out those kids? I knew she was proud, but I also knew that God had each of us, myself and Emma, in two special places, looking out for those who needed help, hope, and most of all, love. Even on my best days, I always needed Emma. With that in my mind, I knew this volunteer crew similarly needed me. Above all else, those kids needed our team of selfless volunteers. It was a humbling thing, feeling a sense of pride in what we were there to accomplish. I closed my eyes as my head sank deeper and deeper into the pillow. All was silent and all was well.

✝

Days two through five were much the same. More frame building. More insulation, pipes, and wires. More plumbing, more drywall, and more painting. It was honestly unbelievable to see just how much went into a single building. To see one giant concrete structure climb fifteen to twenty feet in height and basically come to life, both in size and in structure, was beyond incredible. I had the privilege of being invited over to the local schoolhouse in the early hours of the afternoon on our fifth day to accompany the priest as he taught a lesson about God and love to the children, so that I could actually meet the people who would benefit from our debilitating hours of intense physical labor. As we approached the schoolyard, walking down the sloped gravel path, I was appalled to see that most of the windows were busted out, an old quilt was hanging over the door frame as a makeshift door, and debris was strewn all throughout the high grass surrounding the building. After ducking inside, I was flabbergasted at how small of a living space those children were confined to. There were almost fifty kids packed into the two small classrooms and common area that made up the schoolhouse, all of whom looked at me with curious stares as soon as I entered. I kind of expected it, you know, the "Who the heck is this guy?" look that I got back on my first day working at Palmer Academy. I smiled and waved to the crowd of youngsters as the priest introduced me as the "nice man leading the project of their new home." Almost immediately, the mood shifted, and I began to get some more smiles, nods, and occasionally a rogue high five.

Excited about a new face, they rushed me by storm and gave me the run-down of where they all slept, told me what they did throughout their days, and each spoke their stories of fleeing the old orphanage as it was engulfed by flames. The two counselors' attempts at hushing the children were faulty at first, but soon proved achievable as they circled up the kids, whose ages ranged anywhere from a few months to well into their teen years. As the priest excused himself to begin his short lecture, I casually walked into one of the two classrooms, particularly the room serving as a nursery for the youngest of toddlers, lying peacefully in their makeshift cradles, which appeared to be old, wooden crates padded with rags and pillows. Running my hand along the edge of the crates, completely ignoring the possibility of a splinter, I relished in the quiet snores of the little ones as their soft, almost unnoticeable breaths lifted their chests no less than a centimeter or two.

Nearing the end of the row, I felt a deep chill down my spine, almost as if someone sprayed me with one of those cheap squirt fans that spectators have at outdoor events during the summer. Given the fact that the room was significantly warmer than the temperature that just grazed my vertebrae, I quickly spun around to see if a little kid was messing with me. Much to my surprise, it was just me in that far-from-spacious room, all of the older children still out in the main area, listening to their two counselors and the priest. I went back to inspecting each cradle out of sheer curiosity, but the chill re-emerged almost immediately, on my right shoulder, with what felt like a hand resting just above my collarbone. I was scared to death, but for some unknown reason, it was also kind of soothing. It wasn't just because of the cool refresher from standing in a warm room, but more of a comforting sense. It sounds crazy, and I didn't expect anyone to believe me, but it felt like someone was watching over me. It was as if something, or someone, else was in that room too, but invisible to the naked eye. No matter how hard I tried to put a finger on it, I still found myself confused.

Hesitant as to what any of this could mean, I stood there, frozen. The stone-cold touch never left my shoulder, so I kept thinking to myself, "Emma, if this is you, feel free to knock it off anytime now." I couldn't put my finger on it for certain, but it really did feel like she was there in the

room with me, or at least manipulating me in some way from the "other

side." I collected myself and decided to peer into the last crate before

walking back out to see if the priest was done with his daily words of

wisdom for the kids. What I fell witness to during that very moment would

alter the course of my life forever. It had to have been Emma there, giving

me a sign of some sort. My lackluster belief in God was no more, because it

was precisely then that I realized that He was there with me all along. For in

that chipped shipping crate, laying on a burnt orange colored blanket, was a

baby boy. He couldn't have been any more than a few weeks old, maybe a

month or two at most. His lightly tanned skin was much different from the

pinkish tone I was accustomed to seeing with newborns in America. He was

the only child awake, squeezing his tiny fists around my finger that I

willingly let him take. His soft brown hair looked as if it were just starting to

fill in. But these things aside, it was his eyes that caught me off guard and

sent my voice back into the chambers of my lungs, at a complete and utter

loss for words.

The deep green spheres that stared back into my own were exactly

like Emma's, perhaps identical. That green was purer than the waves of

Alaskan waters and more jaw-droppingly colorful than any painting of Picasso. Never before had I seen that precise shade—the only exception being my best friend, my wife, my purpose in life. I reached down, my stare never breaking contact with those perfectly beautiful orbs. I held this orphaned child in my arms, his weight like that of a thick book, cushioned perfectly in the crook of my folded arms. His tiny palm slowly reached up and out of his nestled place between my forearms and placed his five nubby fingers over my heart. I began to sob. Overwhelmed with the loss of Emma, the flashbacks to almost drinking my life away, my betrayal of God, alienating my family and friends, and the exhaustion from the days prior hit me with a tsunami of emotion. I was consumed with more grief, appreciation, regret, love, and hope in that moment than ever before in my young adult life. Still, amidst my bellowing sobs, this newly birthed child never released his grip on my t-shirt, just above my heart. I sat down in the nearest chair, still dumbfounded at the irony, at the amazing gift of life that I was holding, completely unaware of the fact that a crowd was beginning to form outside the doorway looking in at the weird foreign man hunched over an orphaned Honduran baby with tears streaming down his face. But in that moment, nothing else mattered to me.

In walked the local priest, followed by Pastor McWilliams. Smiles and soggy eyes were both distinguishable on their faces. I put my head back down and closed my eyes, slowly rocking the boy back and forth in my arms. For the first time in over a year, I felt what it was like to hold something so precious in my arms again. I knew that a piece of Emma lay hidden within the heart, mind, and future of this child. By the grace of God, I vowed never to give that up, because I knew that I wasn't going to leave La Colonia without him.

Everyone around me was likely thinking to themselves, "How in the world can this guy just flick a switch and decide that he's going to be a father in a matter of five minutes?" In complete and brutal honesty, it may have been rash. It may have been premature, impulsive, probably even borderline ridiculous. Who was I kidding? It *was* all of those things! But more so than anything else in my life up until that moment, I saw absolutely nothing wrong whatsoever with that decision, and I never have since that very day. While I was working on the final leg of the construction project, I had the volunteers over at the schoolhouse working tirelessly on the proper documentation, making phone calls back to the United States, and reaching out to mutual friends of theirs at the American Consulate. For a process that usually took months or years, we were trying to make it all work out in a mere two days. I would spend my nights at the schoolhouse, rocking him to sleep and telling him stories about Emma and me—about the mom he should have had, the mom he deserved.

I was torn as to what I should name him. I remember looking into his eyes, praying for a name to surface in my mind. It wasn't until the evening before our departure that I was finally handed the proper paperwork to fill out in order to finalize the process. I had to be authorized in both the nations of Honduras and the U.S., but luckily, my history with children was easily reaffirmed by the background checks from my time at Palmer Academy. I was interviewed over the phone by agency workers from the U.S. in addition to a few local officials in Roatan. Apparently, the boy was left at the doorstep of the orphanage with no belongings, no note, no nothing. It sickened me to no end how careless someone could be, to leave their own flesh and blood, only hours into their life, alone and out in the elements. I remember having no faith in the system, doubting that there would be no "pop-ups" in the adoption process or that the transfer would take months, even years to complete, let alone a couple of days.

On the day of the group's departure, I was yet to have the figurative green light to return home with my soon-to-be son. I knew that it meant another few days' worth of lodging, meals, and a later flight home, but I was more than willing to manage the particulars. The new orphanage was flawless by week's end, with all of the volunteers and Pastor McWilliams feeling both exhausted and sore all over. They accomplished so much more than ever anticipated, with the only steps left being some minor fixes, the addition of furniture, and the painting of the two rooms in the back of the building. The outer walls were painted with a flashy coat of light yellow. I was the one who suggested the color, so that heat wouldn't be as absorbed as it would be with a darker color, and once it was done, it truly looked and felt like a home. When I walked in, I could picture the smiles of the children as they soaked up their new atmosphere. I knew that they wouldn't have to worry about the heat because of the new air conditioning unit. I knew that they wouldn't have to worry about the ravages of another fire, because of up-to-date smoke detectors and newly installed electrical wiring with less hazardous material. It made me grateful to feel so safe in this place where such innocent and jubilant kids would be staying until they found their forever families. I recall hugging each of the congregation members before they filed into their shuttle bus to the airport. I could feel their love and appreciation, and with every "thank you," I tried to fight back a tear. If it weren't for them, I would have never been able to find this new beginning or to feel God's magic course through my veins the way it did that day.

I stood there, refusing to let go of Pastor McWilliams, as the chauffeur loaded the bags into the airport van. My tears soaked into her sweaty t-shirt as I kept telling her how much I appreciated her open-mindedness with me, how much I owed Melvin and his mother for their faith in me, and how I knew that God was finally beginning to show me the power of love again. The bus kicked up a cloud of dirt that left me gasping for air as it circled the perimeter of the hotel property and sped off down the road, before disappearing in the crowded alleys of shops and markets downtown. I couldn't wait to go home. The thought of reading stories to my son on our newly painted porch as the lightning bugs lit up the front yard and the hum of the mosquitoes filled our ears filled my heart to capacity. I closed my eyes and saw the two of us playing catch on the baseball diamond down the street, teaching him the basics of the sport I loved so much. I walked upstairs to my room, smiling from ear to ear. I had so much to learn—everything from diapers to baby diets to financial stuff. I knew I was sure to be in way over my head. But as with all things in life, I knew that I would have to be patient and keep an open heart. I knew that Emma would be looking down at me, helping me all the way. I knew that God was going to keep testing me. The weird thing was that I actually felt like I was ready for it. I crawled into bed for a much-needed nap, anxiously awaiting the evening so I could consult with the agency and touch base about the adoption and hold my baby as close to me as I could. It hit me. I was going to name him Emmanuel.

Emmanuel Aparicio Roberts, or Manny for short. A namesake of "Emma Aparicio," I knew it was the perfect tribute to someone who would have been his unbelievably amazing mother. I'm yet to understand how or why the name struck a chord with me that afternoon, but I knew how honored Emma would be. I remembered learning that "Emmanuel" meant "God is with us" when I was in Sunday school as a child however many years ago, which suited our introduction to one another perfectly. I had fulfilled the final promise she asked of me. I, against all the odds, had actually found love once more.

Five more uneventful days came and went, fretting over whether I'd ever gain clearance to fly home with Manny so we could start our lives together in the beautiful suburbs of Baltimore in our cozy home on Shryock Lane. On the fifth morning, I awoke to a phone call in my hotel room around eight o'clock. I answered "¿Hola, quién es?" only to hear an ecstatic, yet recognizable, voice on the other line, with cheering in the background. It was the younger of the two orphanage workers screaming "¡Es oficial! ¡Es oficial!" over and over again. I almost forgot to put on pants before I sprinted down the stairs, refusing to take a chance at the far-from-timely elevator down the hall, and took off down the street to the old school house where the children were playing outside during what would be their final days before moving into the new building. I burst through the entrance right into the arms of the two awaiting orphanage workers, who were jumping up and down with their hands clutching the files of completed paperwork. I gave them each the sloppiest kiss on the cheek as my uncombed, uncharacteristically long hair swung down in front of my eyes before I quickly tucked it back behind my ears.

I scurried back to the room of makeshift cradles and made quiet but extended strides until I reached the last crate, where Manny laid smiling and waving his precious little arms, almost like he was expecting his new dad at any given second. I gently lifted him up and kissed his forehead, holding him closer than ever. Now was not a time for tears, but rather for celebration. I turned to the doorway, bewildered at the crowd of orphans smiling and cheering for Manny and me, almost like a parade procession. To see these kids genuinely happy that one of their own found a family, with no hint of jealousy? I was more humbled than ever before. I walked on over to the middle of the crowd and began singing and dancing with them, my son in my right arm, the adoption files in my left. In all of my life, never have I experienced such a day. I could feel Emma singing and dancing from a far and distant place, too. I bent down and whispered in Manny's ear, a word that he would come to know as love. A word that he would eventually acknowledge as both hope and peace. A word to live each day by. "Always," I whispered. "Always."

✝

It was hard to believe the difficulty of finding a baby carrier, diapers, baby food, baby powder, and clothing all in a three-hour window, especially in the middle of a Honduran town with your ridiculously long flight set to leave by day's end. If anyone were to have seen how flustered and frantic I was on that day, there's no doubt that they would have had themselves a laugh. I couldn't help but imagine how it would all pan out for someone who didn't speak the native language! I finally got Manny strapped into the carrier and finagled the seatbelt buckles in the shuttle bus so we could head off to the airport before our flight left that same evening. A few hundred dollars down the drain in necessities, hotel fees, and an additional plane ticket later, we finally found our seats way back in the far-left corner of a sketchy Boeing 747 with the white paint peeling off the sides. As Emma would have wanted, I sat Manny beside the window so he could look out at the clouds until his eyelids eventually closed and his beautiful green eyes were left out of sight. I followed suit, soon thereafter, while my thoughts drifted and soared from Emma to Manny, to our list, to my family, to the students at the academy, everything.

I knew that I'd need to throw myself back into the ring of life, even more so than I had over the past year or so. I needed to get my life back on track and teach my son that letting your broken heart and distraught mind consume every aspect of your life is the biggest mistake you can make. It's okay to be scared—it's part of being human. It's okay to have your world torn to shreds, because it proves to you the importance of appreciating what you have while you have it. Losing Emma gave me more than it took from me, no matter how hard that was for me to say. I reclined back in my seat as the plane's engines began to rumble and the wheels began to accelerate down the runway. I reached my hand over into the carrier and wrapped my fingers around Manny's tiny fist. I felt his grip, and I smiled. "We're going home, son. We're going home."

Part II

A dogwood petal drifted down from the branch above my head, startling me and sending me falling back onto my backside at the base of the tree. At first, I thought it was a spider, and I probably looked like a total moron as I flailed and swatted around the top of my head until realizing exactly what it was. I must have been crouching here for an hour or so, recollecting the memories and emotions that ultimately brought me to where I am today. It was as if I was in a trance as I sat here, looking down at the aged gravestone and thinking back to all of the love that its engraved name blessed me with during those years of my life. It's so comfortable to sit here with Emma and allow my mind to wander back to those "good ole' days," as well as the bad ones, and everything else in-between. Losing track of time was almost inevitable when I came to visit Emmy. I could sit here for hours on end with my eyes closed, looking back over the past sixteen years of my life without her and how it was as if she were actually with me all along.

Now that I was sitting flat on my rear and still had another hour or so until my shift at work began, I figured I could scoot myself back against the base of the tree and close my eyes for a little while longer. After all, there was still plenty of this beautiful story to recount. I smirked, basking in the shade of this dauntingly magnificent tree and listening to the robins' chirps only feet above my head, hidden within the cover of the leaves.

"Dad, the bus is going to be here any minute! What are you doing in there?" Trying to spread the second and final slice of bread with nutty peanut butter before cramming it into a Ziploc bag, I screamed, "Hold on a minute, I'm going as fast as I freakin' can! Do you have that field trip form for Ms. Singleton?" You'd think that after almost ten full years of taking care of my little one that I would have had the whole "dad" thing down pat. I accidentally sliced the thickest part of my palm with the butter knife as I tried to cram it into the already chock-full dishwasher, which was pretty much the least of my worries on that chaotic morning. With one bloodied hand wrapped up in a dirty napkin and the other holding a poorly assembled lunch box, I came sliding out of the kitchen in a pair of dress socks and wrinkled khakis, tossing the box down the hall to Manny as he scrambled over his untied shoelaces, out the front door, down the porch steps, and across the street after the bus which was already halfway around the corner.

I didn't have the time to sit around and take in just how filthy and unorganized our kitchen had gotten over the course of the past day or two. I had to be at work in ten minutes, even though it was a fifteen-minute drive away, plus I still didn't have a shirt on and I hadn't brushed my teeth yet. Shortly after adopting Manny, I stepped down from my position at Palmer Academy to pursue a more financially suitable job so I could help pay for all of his wants and needs, like any parent in my situation should. If you would have asked him back then, I promise you that he would have called any of his handheld video games a "need" as opposed to a "want," but that's beside my point. I landed a marketing position at a pretty large real estate firm in town and handled all of their advertising, social media campaigns, and directory listings. I cashed in a favor with my new next-door neighbor after helping him unload his trailer when he moved in, so he dialed up his buddy who was the owner of the local firm, and the rest was history.

Every day for those ten years was spent grinding away at work while Manny was at the nursery, then preschool, and then elementary school. By this time in our story, Manny had just turned ten years old and was well on his way to becoming a community sensation on the baseball diamond. Although it was always the sport that held my love the most, I vowed to never push my son in a particular direction in life for my own self-satisfaction. If he wanted to be an artist, play the saxophone, write books, or play sports, I couldn't have cared less. All that mattered to me was that he was happy. He made the decision to join some of his kindergarten classmates in signing up for tee-ball when he was only five years old and he immediately fell in love with the game. I used to sit in my tattered lawn chair, screaming at the top of my lungs whenever he cranked a moonshot well over the head of the centerfielder and casually trotted around the bases and all the way home before the kid could even make his way out to where the ball was. Honest to God, he was nearly better at age five than what I was at fifteen.

I think back to when he picked up one of those beautiful, pearly white, red stitched spheres for the first time. He couldn't have been older than three or four when he was messing around upstairs in my room while I was downstairs making dinner. With the Orioles game blaring in the living room, I was stuck in the kitchen stirring up some sloppy joe sauce when I heard evenly-paced thumps resonating from the staircase. I remember sticking the ladle in the sink and walking over to the bottom of the staircase, only to find an old baseball signed by Brooks Robinson laying there at my feet. Sure enough, Manny stood with the sliest of grins on the top stair, clapping his hands in amusement and giggling at this newly discovered "toy." Not that the little Sandlot recreation in my own home wasn't funny, but I smiled and took the ball back up to my room and stuck it on the top shelf of my closet (which he obviously rummaged through) and made it a priority to get him his own.

Each afternoon when I picked him up from school, he would be standing outside the lobby, staring intently at the far end of the parking lot, trying to make out whether it was my truck he was looking at or not. It was easily the highlight of my day, watching him come sprinting across the front lawn of the school and flinging open the passenger door to my truck. Manny would always make it a habit of telling me the gossip around school for that day, highlighting anything from spilled milk at lunch to someone getting a brush burn on their kneecaps at recess. His stories were adorable and always managed to make me smile. On our way home every day, I'd ask him what his top three favorite parts of the school day were, and I would try and gauge which classes he was enjoying and which ones I would need to try and help him out with more. Just like his old man, he cherished lunch and recess with English and history following closely behind! His weaknesses lied in science and math. I could help him with the elementary level material, but Lord knew that I wouldn't be able to help him as he grew older. I knew it was still a few years away, but I was ecstatic to try and enroll him in a Spanish course. After all, it was in his Honduran blood.

By the time he was six years old, Manny was already well on his way to being a mature and responsible young man, which would have made his mother, Emma, extremely proud. From the time he could speak, I tried my best to instill in him the importance of manners and being polite. He would never refer to an adult as anything other than "sir" or "ma'am," which, although a little outdated, always swooned the elders. "Do unto others what you would hope to be done unto you" was essentially the motto that my son would live by, making me immensely proud. Well, that and "Always." Manny would never hesitate to open a door for anyone or to help unload an old lady's shopping cart if he saw her struggling in the parking lot. It was an honor to call him my son.

One of my proudest moments as a parent was a time when Manny and I were sitting down together in a small pizza shop on the outskirts of town. I was sitting there, intensely concentrating on the towering menu and what I was possibly going to order. I glanced up at Manny, about to ask him what he was hungry for as the waiter would soon be back to take our order. I was surprised to see him sitting there quietly, his head turned at an unusual angle, staring over his shoulder at a man who was sitting by himself in the corner of the room. The elderly gentleman appeared to be somewhere around his latter sixties and had his eyes glued to the diamond-like pattern on the placemat laying before him. "Papa, why is that man sitting alone?" he asked. Unsure as to how I could adequately answer his question, I paused, taking my own look at the old figure cowering in the corner. I noticed that there was only one menu and plate on his table, which led me to believe that he wasn't eagerly awaiting the late arrival of a friend or some partner that was off in the bathroom.

Although sad, I was left with the assumption that the man had recently experienced a loss of some sorts, be it his wife or someone else. I bit my lip, perhaps a little too hard as a small drop of blood coated the tip of my tongue. I saw this as the perfect opportunity to capitalize on my son's curiosity and selfless heart. I had the chance to extend a hand towards someone who seemed to be battling the same enemy—heartbreak—that I once had, and I was not about to let it pass by.

I stood up from my squeaky wooden chair and proceeded to run my fingers through Manny's thick brown hair in passing before I strolled over to the man at the table, whose focus on the placemat was still unmitigated. I startled him as I took the seat across from his on the other side of the table. His eyes darted up at me, and although puzzled, the expression of sheer sadness was painted all across his old and emaciated face. "Excuse me, Sir, but are you waiting on anyone in particular?" I asked. His eyes slowly shifted down towards the placemat again as he ever so slightly shook his head. "My son, Manny, and I would love nothing more than to invite you over to sit with us for lunch. Would you care to join us?" The man looked up at me, shocked at my offer. He looked humbled by it, not offended. A soft "I would love to" escaped his lips as he scooted out of his chair and hobbled over to our table where Manny sat patiently waiting, watching us intently. The man pulled up a chair and introduced himself as Harold McGregor and extended his hand to Manny, which he reluctantly shook. It was remarkable how lively and personable this socially reclusive guy in the corner became in only a few short minutes.

We soon learned that Mr. McGregor had recently lost his wife to a four-year bout with both pancreatic cancer and liver failure. He was only a few short months into the next phase of life, and although it broke my heart to admit, I could relate. He had no children, and his only remaining family lived out in San Diego, so he rarely saw any of them. He served as a Marine in the Vietnam War, which led to one story, then another one, and another three more after that. Unbeknownst to Manny and me (who was listening attentively to every word that Harold said), he was actually a wounded warrior, lifting up the leg of his jeans only to reveal a prosthetic leg. Manny was caught completely off guard! He never asked to touch it, but it was made quite obvious that he'd never seen anything like that before. I had my lips sealed, and every finger crossed, praying that Manny wouldn't say anything along the lines of, "Does this make you a robot?" Much to my satisfaction, he just sat there in amazement.

During the car ride home afterwards, I had to explain that not everyone can just "go out and buy themselves a mechanical leg." He wasn't quite old enough for me to explain the gruesome reality behind why Mr. McGregor had that unique limb of his, but fortunately, he didn't feel the need to ask any further questions. I think that Harold secretly knew about

Emma, although not specifically. After losing her, I found it much easier to pick out people that were feeling the way I once did. He kept casting views in my direction, almost as if to indiscreetly hint at answering why a middle-aged white guy was sitting with a five-year-old Hispanic child in a pizza restaurant all by their lonesome.

You see, up until that point, I had never sat down with Manny and discussed the story of Emma, about his adoption, or about my struggles prior to finding him. I didn't know if telling him that his adoptive father was once an alcoholic was necessarily an appropriate conversation to have before he was even a sixth grader. I didn't know whether his childish innocence clouded the reality that his skin was slightly darker than his dad's or that his hair was much darker, too. Coming into our father-son relationship, I knew with utmost certainty that the both of us would face skepticism and scrutiny towards our ethnic differences, and when the time was right, I would have to have that talk with Manny. From the first day of his adoption, the one word he would hear over and over and over was "Always." After tucking him in each night, it would be, "Always, buddy." "Always, Papa." Before he left for school each morning, the same would hold true. He never asked why that was "our thing" or where it came from, but in due time, I knew that he would learn.

Our meal ended on a high note as Harold offered to pay the bill, much to my opposition, thanking us for our selfless invitation before we parted ways. "God would be proud of us," I thought to myself as I walked hand-in-hand with Manny out to the truck. He jumped up and buckled himself in before we drove to the baseball field at the local park where we would toss and work on hitting drills before dinner later that evening. Lying in bed that night, I struggled to close my eyes and dream because of my fear of telling Manny about my life before him. This was an obstacle that I'd seen in movies, but I had absolutely no idea as to how I should go about explaining it all. But, that was a battle for another day, and I had enough time to think about it before making any rushed, impulsive decisions. I rolled over to the cold side of the pillow, allowed the weight of my eyelids to take over, and drifted off into a deep slumber, wishing Emma's hair was still tickling my face as I slept.

Manny's final year of elementary school and first year of middle school flew by; his success in baseball continued to soar to ridiculous heights and showed no signs of slowing down. By the time he was beginning his seventh-grade year, he was well on his way to becoming a legitimate college prospect. He had shot up in height to about 5'10", which was only a few inches shorter than me. More so than that, he was sitting comfortably at around 80 mph across the diamond from shortstop. I had never played the middle infield in my life, but as a catcher growing up, I was pretty well versed on how each position was supposed to be played and how to succeed regardless of where you were on the baseball diamond. Through his tee-ball and little league years, he tried getting a feel for which position he wanted to try and move forward with as he grew older. Sure enough, the typical "captain's position" suited him well, and every day after school he wanted nothing more than to go practice for hours on end before the sun went down and it was time to wrap up his schoolwork before snoozing. He couldn't have been older than nine when he had mastered everything there was to learn about shortstop.

As ridiculous as it seems, he got so accustomed to crushing pitching as a right-handed hitter that he decided to give left-handed hitting a fair chance too, although that was a lot easier said than done. As someone who has been around the game for decades, I was thoroughly convinced that he had a gift and a natural talent in the sport, perhaps more so than anyone I'd ever seen before, my personal bias aside. He knew that his faith, then his family and friends, his grades, and then baseball would cap off his list of priorities. Our summers would be spent traveling up and down the eastern seaboard playing on his tournament team, where they'd demolish nearly every opponent that they played. Manny had no problem turning heads, diving for groundballs up the middle, planting his right knee on the edge of the infield dirt, spinning, and throwing a missile across the field to get the runner, regardless of how fast they ran. We couldn't go anywhere without someone asking him to come to play for their team, trying to convince him to play for another program, questioning his birth certificate, and seeing if he was getting any recruitment looks yet.

At tournaments, the parents and I would chuckle when the opposing team's spectators would make comments about it being "unfair" or that Manny was "not even close to being eligible." Word on the street was that the high school coach already knew his name and was looking at him as someone who could lead his varsity team to a promising record, and he wasn't even a teenager yet! I tried to teach him that being humble was going to be his secret weapon if he wanted to continue progressing in the game of baseball. His closest friends came from his little league and tournament teams, and I couldn't have been happier with how well they all got along. It was incredible to see him having fun while simultaneously working his butt off and building relationships centered around the little white ball with red seams. I never wanted to be viewed as one of those helicopter parents who drove their child to sheer exhaustion with practice and whatnot, but this was all on Manny. In balancing his academics, extra-curricular activities, and baseball, getting even better and perfecting his craft was pretty much his drug.

It was late May of that very same seventh-grade season when it happened. Manny had a little more than two weeks of school left at the time, but his mind was well into the realm of summer vacation. Trust me, his grades were beginning to reflect it, no matter how many conversations we had about the importance of not slacking off. That Friday, I sat in the parking lot of the middle school, waiting for him to come bolting out the entrance doors, excited for the car ride down to Harrisonburg, Virginia where his weekend tournament was set to take place. The trip, including a few pee breaks and fast food pit stops, took us around four hours to complete and brought us to the hotel around eight o'clock that night. Manny's team was scheduled to play a handful of pool play games that Saturday, which would dictate their standing for advancement come Sunday morning. If my recollection is treating me well, Manny played a respectable game early Saturday morning. He was flawless, almost like an artist with his defense out at shortstop. He struggled during his first couple of at-bats, but figured out the minor kink in his swing in the batting cage beside the field before game two.

The second game began only a few short hours after our narrow victory earlier in the day. As per usual, Manny was penciled into the lineup as the starting shortstop and hitting leadoff in the batting order. The opposing team drew a ton of stares, towering over my son and his closest buddies by three or four inches at least. If any of these bearded children were to claim themselves as a father, I wouldn't have had a hard time believing it! I think that word must have spread to the other team about Manny's skill and some of his recent accolades, which must not have sat well with their squad, seeing as though they wanted to be the only "hot shots" that weekend. My kid wasn't a hot shot. He was grounded, sportsmanlike, humble, and let his time on the field speak for itself, which I knew would serve him well as both a baseball player and as a young man. I sat in the solace of my four-legged sling chair down the third base line, my kneecaps only inches from the fence. The burly boys from the other team were watching Manny go through his normal stretching and fielding routines in the outfield grass. I watched as their focus hardened on Manny, whispering back and forth to each other and cracking sly grins. Manny hated attention, so I knew it was going to get on his nerves if the other team kept acting so juvenile and antagonistic. I'm sure that Manny picked up on the childishness of things, but as with every game he played, his mind was too entranced by the game, so nothing was going to sneak through his inner ears and throw him off.

Leading off the top of the fourth inning, Manny's hard grounder between the third base and shortstop hole proved to be enough to break up the opposing pitcher's no-hitter. Frustrated about giving up his first base hit of the ballgame, the behemoth right-hander slammed the rosin bag to the ground and viciously dug his new Nike cleats into the rubber mound, all the while reddening in the face. It was comical, seeing this youngster with such an enormous stature show the self-control of his actual age. Manny strode

out to a daring lead, his weight planted on the balls of his feet. Anticipating a

game with very few baserunners, Manny extended his secondary lead as

soon as the pitcher delivered, sending both the catcher and pitcher into high

alert for a potential steal. Now, even when things in my life came across as

peachy, dandy, whatever word you want to use, they were often gilded, and

the tides would drastically turn sooner rather than later. Oddly enough, that

was one of those times. "Meat," the name a few of the parents jokingly

assigned to the kid on the mound, could hardly focus on the batter, casting

long stares over his shoulder at my son on first base. Itching to swipe a bag,

Manny added another step and a half to his already notable lead. In a blur of

movement, Meat's back foot stepped off the mound as he hurled the ball

over to first base in a frantic attempt at picking off Manny.

Pivoting on his left foot, Manny dove back to first base with his arms

fully extended and dirt caking his chin. The ball was considerably off target

and much lower than intended, merely two or three inches off the ground.

What should have been a playable ball by the first baseman suddenly turned

painful as it bounced off the infield dirt and hit Manny's elbow as he lay

fully extended with his fingers gripping the base. He immediately began to writhe in pain, grasping his right elbow and rolling around on the ground. I instinctively flung open the dugout gate and sprinted over to where the umpires, coaches, and several players were congregated over my boy. Sure, I've had my fair share of bee stings, bruises, and welts over the years of parenting, but I had no idea how to handle whatever was about to come of that.

Kneeling down over Manny, I could see his now calmed body shaking oh so slightly, and he looked up at me with those piercing green eyes and whispered, "I'm scared, Papa." His left hand was clutching his right elbow, yet not a single tear managed to stream down his face. Everyone who was huddled around was annoyingly persistent in their questions, and I could tell that Manny was too in shock to allow anything to penetrate his eardrums. I reached down and cradled him as if he was a little kid again, but he was a whole lot heavier than I expected. Parents from both sides of the field ran over to share their good wishes as I carried him in the direction of the parking lot, where we would drive immediately to the nearest hospital. Manny laid down in the backseat with his eyes closed, still gripping his right elbow. Pulling up to the turnaround in front of the First Star Medical Clinic, I tried to help Manny even though he wanted to walk in on his own accord while a kindhearted valet gentleman took my keys and drove my car to the temporary lot.

Thoroughly agitated at how much paperwork I needed to complete before they'd be able to send Manny back to the assessment room, I viciously flipped from page to page in their insurance packet, carelessly scribbling my name wherever I spotted a highlighted dotted line. Sending him immediately to the x-ray room, the medical staff left me alone with my head in my hands, sitting just outside the technology-filled evaluation space. Manny and the nurse emerged soon after that, his face looking more and more distraught as time went on. My hand was grasping his as we waited patiently for the doctor on call to enter the room, spill the beans, and do whatever we had to in order to get back to the way things were just over an hour ago.

An elderly man in an oversized lab coat came into the room after knocking on the door two short times, introducing himself as the lead surgeon for the orthopedic department. Plopping down onto the ergonomic chair in front of the computer, he began clicking through file after file on the desktop until an x-ray of a bent elbow appeared. Right at the base of the elbow, I saw what looked like a chip of bone that detached from the rest of the main bone; sure enough, that was indeed the fact of the matter. Apparently, the ball had hit a weak spot on the elbow and caused it to break instantly. The catch—probably not the best word choice in this case—was that there was actually a tendon attached to the small fragment of bone, which made the injury even edgier. Manny's tears streamed the whole way down his colorless cheeks, falling silently onto his dirt-stained jersey.

I stood up and hugged him as tightly as I ever had, running my hands through his thick head of hair as the doctor sat, watching sympathetically. "I'm sorry to be the one who has to break this news to you, son." The doctor (whose voice was surprisingly high-pitched) unbuttoned the top of his white coat, brushing some sweat off his forehead with his sleeve. "Based off of what I'm looking at here, you've got a fairly clean break," he said while moving his pen in a circular motion around the x-ray image. "Fortunately, the detached fragment is close enough to the bone that I don't think you're going to need surgery. If the broken piece were any farther away from the elbow from what it is now, we'd have to utilize a screw insertion to reconnect the two pieces. As it stands, our best bet is to immobilize your arm for a few months so we can let that fragment reattach itself to the main bone all on its own."

I was hoping the news would at least perk Manny up a little bit, seeing as though he wouldn't need surgery and have a screw in his elbow for life. The question was all over his face, almost like a mask. The surgeon caught on quickly, turning his eyes to my boy, scooching himself a foot closer to Manny. Resting his hand on Manny's knee, the doctor whispered "Yes, buddy, your baseball career is going to be put on hold for a couple of months. If you listen to my instructions and are willing to be patient, I promise that by the end of August, you'll be able to start swinging a bat and throwing lightly again." Manny lifted his left arm and wiped the tears from his eyes, nodding in agreement. We stood up and shook hands, bidding the doctor farewell and thanking him for his time before a new nurse arrived to wrap up Manny's arm from his wrist the whole way to his lower bicep.

Per the nurse's timeline, he would have to wear the hard cast for four weeks before needing to change to the limited range-of-motion brace, kind of like those weird robotic things that football players wear on their knees. He'd also have to go through a few weeks of physical therapy to rebuild the strength and range of motion in his arm, but if all worked out according to plan, there was a chance he'd be able to play in the last few games of his fall baseball season. It was Manny's first time in a cast, so I tried to make light of the situation by popping the cap off a marker at the checkout counter and signing "Padre" on his upper forearm. Cracking a smile, he muttered some comment about getting the team and girls back at school to sign it too, which made me feel relieved to see his faith in the process. On the car ride home, I reminded him that God wouldn't put us through anything we couldn't handle and that there would be a lot of good, although I wasn't entirely sure of what, that would come of it all. Sitting in the back seat of the truck, Manny nodded oh so slightly before leaning his head against the window, closing his eyes, and drifting off to sleep.

The next few months would prove to be emotionally complicated and mentally exhausting. Manny was pretty much on lock-down because of his arm, doing his best to write and stay competent in the final weeks of the school year. He'd spend long hours sitting alone in his room each night, flipping through TV channels and trying to forget the limited range of mobility holding him back from doing his typical routines, especially practicing the game he loved most. I had cut back on my hours at the firm and enrolled myself in classes at a small community college down the road from our house, which meant I pulled into the driveway sometime in the evening most days of the week.

Given that baseball was what he lived for, the time spent alone at home and away from the baseball diamond began to eat away at him, almost like a junkie struggling to cope with a rehab stint. Instead of looking at each day as one step closer to being back in action, Manny saw it as yet another day in the wasteland of boredom and sadness. It tore him apart on the inside and he'd refuse to talk about it most nights, blocking me out in any way he could. As a dad, it was extremely tough to see my son suffer through this, but the hardest part was knowing that any attempt at cheering him up would be for naught. When I did his laundry, I could see just how many tear stains covered his pillow case. If baseball wasn't an active part of his life, he never really seemed to think about too much else.

By now, it was late June, so Manny's school year had already been over for a couple of weeks. I walked into the house, my backpack slung over my left shoulder and a bag of Chinese take-out in my left hand. "Food's here," I yelled as I slid off my shoes and tossed my keys onto the one spot on the kitchen counter that wasn't covered by envelopes, dirty dishes, and appliances. Waiting for a response that never seemed to come, I set my bags on the floor and walked into the living room, only to find everything as I last

saw it—lights off, pillows positioned neatly, and couches left empty.

Puzzled, I walked upstairs to Manny's room and flicked on the light.

Miscellaneous notes and books from his summer homework were stacked

inches high on the desk, a fallen pile scattered across the floor. His lamp

light was on, casting a glow over a plate with a half-eaten peanut butter and

jelly sandwich right beside his first ever home run ball. Starting to worry, I

ran into the bathroom—no Manny. Flinging open the door to my room, a

sense of relief jolted through me to see him sitting on the far side of my bed,

his back to me, facing the wall, his eyes looking down at something small in

his hands.

    I walked over slowly, still reasonably confident that he knew I was

there. Squinting at what he was holding (all the while pondering what he was

doing in my room), I sat myself down beside him and put my hand on his

shoulder. Appalled, I stared blankly at the list that Emma and I had written at

the Bay so many years ago, gripped in his fingers, half of it crossed out in

thick scribbles of pen, half of it left undone, a memory that'd been pushed to

the deepest confines of my mind for years and years. "Papa, what is this?" I

was partially disappointed at the fact that his curiosity (or rather, his boredom) led him to rummage through my belongings in the back of my nightstand. "Who is Emma? Was she my mom?" It was as if someone sucked all of the air out of the room at that very moment. I'd put off the inevitable for years, trying to convince myself that I'd be able to handle that time when it came. Oh, how wrong I was.

Manny's glacier-green eyes stared into mine, begging for an answer that I wasn't entirely sure how to give. Gently, I took the list from his hands and began scanning over the things left unchecked: an overseas voyage to Greece, a food fight, steal free samples, and a handful of other silly feats that had escaped my mind since the love of my life had passed away. "Follow me," I said, reaching back into my nightstand to grab a scrapbook of our most precious moments together, telling our story from our time in high school, through college, her battle, the impromptu wedding, all of it. Tucking it under my arm with my hand still on Manny's shoulder, I nudged for him to make his way downstairs. The silence wasn't as awkward as it may sound, making our way down the steps and into the living room.

I sat the book down on the coffee table before walking into the kitchen to grab the little white Chinese take-out boxes from the bag and a fork for each of us. Manny's hands were folded, his eyes gazing aimlessly at the floor, then the table, then the window. Sticking a fork into one of the boxes, puncturing a piece of golden General Tso's chicken, I handed it to Manny. By that point, he had mastered the use of his left hand in writing and eating. Given the fact he was a switch hitter, being well-versed with both hands was almost a necessity. "We met in high school," I started off by saying. I sat, reminiscing about our perfect story, walking through my life with Emmy, my journey into the abyss, and my revival in finding love again. Taking an occasional bite of dinner, I told my son about how we first met, about Ms. Blair and Robbie, and about that evening out on the Chesapeake when we decided to make our "couples' bucket list." I shared the story about our commentary in the grocery store and our adventures out on the water, Orioles games, everything. Manny's attentiveness grew as the night grew longer, cracking a grin at the comical stories, and looking solemn when hearing about her fight with breast cancer. Finding love again, taking care of her aunt and brother, and never losing my faith in God were the three promises I made to her before she took her last breath, and I shared that with Manny.

I divulged the darkness and depression that plagued me for months after she was gone, then about my comeback and the mission trip where I found him. I told him about how his eyes and Emma's eyes were the same, and that it wasn't a coincidence, but rather God's magic and guidance in full swing on that day at the orphanage. "You're the love that found me, son. You're my second chance, and the reason we've been put on this Earth is to love and grow together, to be here for each other like no other father and son have ever been before." Although visibly exhausted, he nodded his head and eventually leaned in for a hug. A tear streamed down my right cheek, landing in Manny's thick head of hair that I was running my fingers through. I could feel Emma's presence in the room, smiling at how my life had evolved since she joined God's army of angels. I squeezed Manny even tighter.

About a week or two after our talk, Manny's hard cast was off and on came the range-of-motion brace. It was funky looking; there was a dial on the side of it with a pin that could be moved to accommodate a wider angle as his physical therapy sessions loosened up his reattached tendon. He was aggravated enough that he wasn't able to play, but the fact that he had to wake up early three times a week for me to take him into the therapy facility before my classes started annoyed him even more. His days at home consisted of watching hours' worth of daytime baseball games on TV, doing left-hand swings off of a tee into a net in the backyard, and failing miserably at trying to teach himself how to throw left-handed. If professional athletes rarely attempted to learn how to throw with the opposite arm, I wasn't entirely sure why Manny was convinced he could be the lone exception. He was a dreamer, though, and I would never stop him from chasing his endeavors, no matter how big.

If the weather wasn't too brutally hot, he'd walk down the street to Javier's house, and the two of them would walk together to the little league field about a half mile away, lugging a bat and a bucket of balls. Javy, a slightly overweight kid who caught for Manny's tournament team, could practice his throws to second base where Manny could straddle the bag, make the catch with his glove hand, and apply a fake tag as if an invisible runner were sliding in head-first. Returning the favor, Javy would hit ground balls to Manny at shortstop. Although he couldn't throw, he'd field the ball, practice his footwork, and drop the ball into the bucket. Since Javy was healthy and able to play every weekend, he wasn't always up to the extra practice throughout the week, leaving Manny high and dry at home alone until I could get there in the early evening to take over in his place. During

weeks that we didn't eat too much takeout, we'd venture into the city and

snag two of the cheapest nose-bleed seats at Camden Yards we could find

and make our way down to the lower sections, evading any ushers we saw.

I never once prided myself on my cooking skills, but I was

determined on turning that evening's meal into the best of the week, maybe

even the best of the month. Stirring the kettle that was filled with thick red

sauce and meatballs for my attempt at a spaghetti dinner, I called for Manny

to come downstairs to eat. The noodles were still steaming in the strainer as

he dragged his feet like cinder blocks down the steps, through the living

room, and into the kitchen. I could tell that something was wrong, just by the

way he was sulking and not saying anything. His mood had gradually gotten

better over the course of the past however many weeks, so it was easy to

notice that he wasn't his usual self. I sat his plate down in front of him and

pulled up a seat across the table. "Did you make it out to practice with Javy

today?" Shaking his head, he gazed down at his plate where his fork was pushing around a meatball. He looked uninterested, the farthest thing from hungry, and utterly dejected.

"What's wrong?" I asked. Continuing to stare down at his heaping plate of pasta, Manny muttered something quietly under his breath and began to fidget with his arm brace. "What?" I asked again, this time more assertive. Again, he muttered something under his breath, just barely louder than before. Growing more agitated, I raised my voice and belted out, "What the heck are you saying? Speak up!" In a swift movement of his left arm, Manny swatted the plate off the table, sending it to the floor in hundreds of broken pieces of glass. The sauce sprayed across the living room carpet, the noodles and meatballs left in a toppling mound amidst the shards of glass. "Is Emma the only reason you adopted me? Do you even love me, or is this just one of your stupid promises to her now that she's dead?" His cheeks were red with anger, his eyes welling up with tears. He bent down, taking a handful of spaghetti off the floor into his left hand and reared back before launching it in my direction, hitting me square in my chest.

Speechless at what had just transpired, I stood there motionless, watching as he bolted up the stairs, sobbing hysterically, and slammed the door behind him after going into his room. That was completely uncharacteristic of him, the literal opposite of how he acted throughout the duration of his young life to that point in time. It was as though all of the will power in my legs evaporated and I collapsed to the floor, landing almost directly on a pile of glass and Italian goodness. Crying to that extent was reintroduced to me. I was bawling, the tears flooding out of my eyes and the snot running out of my nose. It was horrific and quite possibly an even bigger breakdown than anything I had endured during the aftermath of losing my wife. To see that raw emotion in my son, the person on Earth who I loved more so than anyone or anything else, act so vulnerable and enraged was heart-wrenching. And to know that he was under the impression that my feelings for him were nothing more than an extension of those for Emmy? It was far more than what I could have ever expected to handle in taking on this role as an adoptive father.

I must have been cross-legged on the floor with my head in my hands for no less than an hour, shaken by the words and actions of Manny and dating myself back to the loss of my best friend. The deep red stains of that night's dinner had begun to set in, ruining my shirt and leaving a promising expense for needing new carpet. The all-too-familiar creak of the second-to-last step penetrated my ears, and I lifted my head up slowly from an empty gaze at the floor. Standing on the staircase, his eyes visibly irritated and watery, Manny cast a glance my way in the living room. He made his way down to where I sat and reluctantly plopped himself down to my left, before putting his braced arm around my right shoulder. "Papa, I'm sorry. I know that doesn't fix it, but I'm really, really sorry for saying what I did and for doing something this stupid." Beginning to cry, he buried his head in his shirt, and heavy breathing soon followed.

"I will never be able to express to you how much I love you, my son—never. I can't expect for you to understand what I went through before you came into my life. Emma was my everything. She was my best friend and the love of my life. Yes, my child, there is so much beauty and striking similarity between you both, but no, not once have I ever said or done something with you just for the sake of making myself feel better about losing her. Have I ever lied to you?" I whispered, teary-eyed. A muffled "No" escaped the inside of his shirt. "What have I told you all along about everything being God's plan?" This time silent, he merely nodded, sniffling his emotions back into his body. "You are my everything. You're the reason I wake up every single day with a smile on my face. You're the same reason I go to bed with one on my face, too. I think about you when I'm in class, when you're at school, and whenever you aren't by my side. You're more than a son, you're like a best friend, little brother, and son all in one. You'll never find a bigger cheerleader or someone who will scream louder until their lungs hurt when you're up to bat or make a play out in the field. You're my kid, I'd be shocked if you didn't overthink things as much as what you do. You're like your dad."

"It sucks," Manny said as he pulled his shirt down from over his face, wiping his eyes on his sleeve. "I didn't mean what I said. This summer sucks, and I'm always so sad and bored. All I ever do anymore is sit in my room and think about everyone being able to play except for me, about you and me, about a lot of things. I just want my arm to be strong again. And I think about your life with Emma, and I just want you to be that happy with me, too." I understood his pain, both mentally and emotionally. I fulfilled the promise to Emmy of finding love again, but I knew that God took me by the hand and led me over to that final cradle in the orphanage on purpose.

Emma's love never waned, and I always knew when she was there in the room watching over Manny and me. This was one of those times. I pushed myself up off the stained floor, stepped over Manny's extended legs, and made my way over to the towering mound of spaghetti noodles and meatballs. Crouching down, I scooped up two of the meat chunks which were cold by then, yet still covered in sauce, into my palm. Pulling my arm backward, I slung the two meatballs at Manny, both of which hit him square in the chest, instantly ruining his light-yellow shirt. That was one of the few times I couldn't pinpoint the expression on his face. Was it confusion? Was it fear? Was it disbelief? When my handful of noodles came flying almost directly into the center of his face, his jaw dropped. "What the heck was that for?" he asked. I apologized, "I'm sorry, but you can't just expect to be let off the hook with this one!"

Kicking the plate remnants into the kitchen area, I tossed him a few meatballs, which he instinctively put into his right hand before realizing he was still on the disabled list. Saying nothing, I closed my eyes, stuck my arms out like a cross, and waited. If there was one thing I knew about him, it was that he'd never shy away from a free shot, let alone a messy one. I felt the first meatball hit me in my left ribcage, obviously off target from wherever he was aiming because of needing to use his left arm instead. I smiled, even after the second and the third pelted my right shoulder and my left temple, respectively. I launched more noodles his way, missing poorly and splattering them all over the couch. Acrobatically, I dodged a fistful of soaring pasta which went right over my head and hit the wall behind me.

Two minutes felt like ten seconds, and we collapsed in laughter, gripping our

sides in pain at how hysterically we were chuckling.

Manny leaned over and rested his head on my shoulder. Withdrawing

my wallet, I reached into the back compartment and unfolded an old,

wrinkly piece of paper with "Maryland State Boating Commission" faded on

the outer side of the crease. I opened up the sheet, revealing a partially

completed bucket list—the same one Manny had stumbled across only a

week or two earlier. I looked into his curious eyes, instantly reminding me of

the mom he should have had. I took my index finger and ran it through the

thick layer of tomato sauce on the arch of his nose before using it to strike a

chunky, red line through "food fight" halfway down the page. "I love you,

buddy." "I love you too, Papa. Always?" "Always." I smiled, looking around

at the absolute mess that was the room around me. "I never really cared too

much for the look of this room, anyway." "Yeah, neither did I."

That very evening opened the door to what were easily some of most

exciting and heartwarming months of my life. As for Manny, I know he'd say the same. Still juggling a full schedule of classes and working part-time, I made an effort at pushing my take-home assignments off until Manny was long asleep. Ever since our food fight, we started ramping up his physical therapy routine so as to reach his goal of being able to throw again before his first day back to school, pushing the limits of the doctor's timeline. Every day before work or class, I rolled Manny out of bed just after 6:00 a.m. for our daily run. Scarfing down a granola bar, he'd lackadaisically string together his shoelaces, and we'd walk off the front porch, out to the sidewalk, and take off down the block. In some of my classes, I learned all about the cardiac system and blood circulations (thrilling stuff, really), so I tried to use that in a way that would get more blood to Manny's arm before doing some stretching exercises, while also keeping him in shape.

No matter how many times I scolded him, he never seemed to be able to pull himself away from the TV screen throughout the course of the days when he was home alone, so I had to push him a little bit extra when I had the chance. Earbuds in, I'd always find some way to make him laugh while on our run, whether it was my excessive use of the air guitar or my obnoxiously loud voice belting out whatever song was ringing throughout my ears. Once we hit the end of the block, we'd pop a left and cut through a backyard, taking us down an old beaten path in the neighboring patch of woods before reaching a set of railroad tracks that stretched for about a mile and a half. It was serene, honestly. The sun would rise and shine through the gaps in-between the trees, lighting up the railroad and all the dew on the surrounding weeds. Taking another shortcut through the same patch of woods, we would make our way out to an opening in the brush that butted right up against the outfield wall of his soon-to-be high school's baseball field.

Sometimes we'd stop for a breather and talk about high school ball, or maybe even run a few sprints on the diamond if we were unusually awake. We'd eventually jog our way back home before I grabbed a shower and had to head out the door. Manny, to no surprise at all, would typically crawl back into bed to catch another few hours of shut-eye.

Not too long after our food fight, I began to take notice of the fact that Manny was growing significantly more interested in learning about Emma. It was almost every day that he'd ask me a question about her, or about what else was on that list tucked away in my wallet. It pained me, knowing that the number of stories I was able to share wasn't nearly as much as what I would have hoped. Our fairytale life together was short-lived. I had always believed that there was no such thing as a happy ending to our story until Manny came along. You see, at that point in my life, I was so disgustingly ignorant and refused to turn the page. When I did, however, I then realized that I hadn't even begun the sequel to the story called "loss."

Nearing the end of that July, I went out on a limb and made the most financially irresponsible, spontaneous, and yet indisputably the greatest decision of my life. I managed to get an excused absence from my classes for a week's time and used the remainder of my sick days for the year at the firm. I took what was perhaps the most inconceivable chunk out of my already subpar savings account and dished out a few thousand dollars, which I desperately needed to put towards a new truck that had less than 200,000 miles on it, without thinking twice. Getting in touch with Javy's parents, I devised a plan for the two boys to get together and head to the field, something that had become much more common by that point since Manny was beginning to throw lightly again. In Manny's mind, I was working diligently in class, learning all about procedures, anatomy, etc. In reality, I was scrambling around the house, making phone calls to the neighbors asking them to keep an eye on the house for the next week, texting

classmates to send me make-up work, and stuffing anything that a teenage

boy would need over the course of a week into our two tiny suitcases.

Praying to God that I didn't miss a toiletry, I threw the two overly-

crammed suitcases into the back of my truck and drove down the street to

the field, thankful to see the boys playing catch on the infield grass. I honked

from the parking lot as I peered down the leftfield foul line, making them

both spin around in surprise. They hustled over to my driver's side window,

immediately asking, "What're you doing here?" "I got out of class early

today, and I figured you might want to go on a little adventure. Mind if I

borrow him for a little bit, Javy?" The two turned towards each other,

shrugged, and walked back to the dugout to grab their gear before parting

ways. Stepping up and into the passenger seat, Manny asked, "Where are we

going?" as he struggled to get the seatbelt unpinned from his closed truck

door. Smirking, I said, "To go get some groceries." Calling my bluff,

annoyance spread across his face. I guess when you've spent almost every

day with one parent your entire life, it becomes second nature to know when

they're fibbing. "Sure, we are." Crossing his arms, he stared straight through

the windshield, doing his best to figure out where we were heading.

I flicked my right-hand turn signal on, merging into the right lane just as we drove beneath the "BWI Airport" sign overlooking the highway. Doing my absolute best to keep the secret, I refused to allow any hint of emotion to creep onto my poker face. Out of the corner of my eye, I could see Manny making short, periodic glances in my direction, hoping that I'd let up even a little bit about this so-called "adventure." It was when I turned down a street labeled "long-term parking" that he knew something major was up. "What are we doing here? Are we meeting someone? Are we going somewhere? Where are we going? I don't have a suitcase or anything. This isn't funny, seriously, why are we here?'' Pulling into a parking spot that appeared to be no less than a mile away from the airport, I turned to him, raising my index finger and putting it over his lips, politely urging him to hush. I asked, "Can you hand me my wallet out of the glove box?"

Fighting with the rusted handle, he yanked it open and tossed me my wallet. "Can you get me a pen? There should be one behind all those registration papers." With papers spilling onto the floor, he rustled his hand into the back of the compartment and withdrew an old pen that was missing a cap. With imaginary fingers crossed inside my head, hoping that the pen still had ink, I opened up my wallet, took out Emma's list, unfolded it, and spread it out on the dashboard, right in front of Manny. His eyes were glued to the pen in my hand as I took it through the line that simply read "Greece." A look of astonishment covered his face as he gasped, ripping the list out of my hand to make sure his eyes weren't fooled. I unbuckled my seatbelt, reached over, and gave him an emotional hug, doing everything in my power not to shed a single tear. "Two down, eight more to go." Stretching his seatbelt as far as it could go, he wrapped his arms around me. "Always, Papa." "Always, buddy."

Flagging down a shuttle, the two of us excitedly jumped on board and grabbed two seats in the second row, right beside an older couple who looked less-than-enthusiastic about how loudly Manny kept repeating to himself, "We're going to Greece, we're going to freaking Greece! Emmy wouldn't believe that we're actually doing this, no way." I would have paid far more than a few thousand dollars to get that type of reaction on camera. Priceless? Ha, to say the least! I couldn't help but think to myself how clutch of a move it was to have Manny's passport picture taken last year, just in case we'd ever have to go back to Honduras for any reason. By the grace of

God, our suitcases weighed just under the maximum allowance, and we headed off to security. Not having flown since his trip to the United States as a newborn, Manny was exuberant about having to take off his shoes, belt, and putting his iPod in one of the little gray containers. The TSA agents smiled as they waved him through the metal detector, picking up on the fact that it was his first real travel experience.

The sweet old security lady responsible for the pat-downs winked at me before whispering, "It never gets old!" as I bent down to tie my shoes, pointing to Manny who was staring in amazement at all the stores, the gigantic planes outside the window, and the long treadmills on the floor. "It's going to be a long seven days—that I can promise you!" I said before picking up my carry-on bag and walking over to Manny. Our flight was scheduled to leave at 4:00 p.m., and it would take almost twelve hours to get there. I made sure to bring extra chargers so his iPod wouldn't die and I downloaded a few movies on my tablet so he wouldn't get excruciatingly bored on the way over. I told him that Emma would have fought me for the window seat and that she would want more than anything for him to have it instead. I wasn't paying attention, so when the flight attendant scolded

Manny about having his lap tray down before takeoff, I told him it was my fault and not to worry about it.

The acceleration of the plane pushed Manny's tall teenage frame back into his cushioned seat, his stare still fixated out the window as we took to the air and soared above the city of Baltimore. "Look, I think I see Camden Yards!" He pointed down at the city, which was almost the size of a speck by the time I could peak my head over his shoulder. I thought back to when it was the two of us together, flying into that next chapter of our lives all those years ago. The seat to my right was empty, oddly enough. I reached over and fastened the seatbelt, pretending as if Emma was sitting there with us. "I'm sorry, I'll take the aisle seat on the way home," I jokingly said to her inside my head. I reclined my seat, closed my eyes, and drifted off to sleep.

We arrived in Athens just under the estimated flight time, both of us brutally exhausted and sore from being confined to our spots for almost half of a day. After making sure not to leave anything on the plane, we limped down the stairs near our terminal to baggage claim, exchanging a loud high-five once we saw our two checked suitcases and knew they didn't get lost in transit. The two of us boarded a bus outside the airport that took us on a half-hour trip through the most beautiful landscape we'd ever seen. It was surreal, stepping off the bus out in front of our hotel on the complete other side of the world. I can't tell you how many times we found ourselves speechless, gasping at the scenery around us and taking in all of the sights, sounds, and smells that overtook our senses. Following check-in, we collapsed onto our beds, our spines thanking us for the chance to recuperate after the long flight. Since it was just after 11:00 a.m. Athens time, we voted on taking a short nap before showering and heading out to explore the city and get a bite to eat.

Our tentative plan, thanks to my brilliant Googling skills only a few weeks prior, was to spend Saturday through Monday in Athens, catch a train, travel south until we hit water, and jump on a boat that would take us to Mykonos. We'd stay there Tuesday through Wednesday, before one last boat ride to Santorini, where we'd fly out of on Friday evening to head home. Manny was awestruck by the size of the Parthenon, soaking in the words of a tour guide that we followed closely throughout the day. We didn't pay, but we slipped into the crowd unnoticed! We learned all about the Greek gods and about Athens' unique background since some of the earliest years in human history. Venturing throughout the city limits, we made sure to visit the Acropolis, the Temple of Olympian, and Philopappos Hill. Our feet ached by the end of each day's activities, but it was worth it. Hearing Manny read off some of the ridiculous facts listed in some of the hotel's tourist brochures was fantastic. Proclaiming himself as our official tour guide, he led the way from one iconic location to another.

He had actually learned a lot about Greece in his seventh-grade ancient civilizations class, which made the trip even more special. "I can't believe just how old all of these monuments are. It's like walking around a museum the size of a city, can you even imagine what it would be like to live here?" Walking through an old chapel on the final leg of the tour, we made it a point to sit down and say a prayer, thanking God for all of the beautiful years we had shared together, asking that He and His angels take care of Emma for us, and expressing our wishes for safe voyages over the course of the week. To think that I had once despised God and blamed him for all of my hardships embarrassed me. By then a firm believer in God having a plan for everything and everyone, I remember feeling grateful for finding that light again and for keeping that promise to Emmy.

Mykonos was breathtakingly pretty, and I can speak for Manny and myself when I say that it was our favorite of the three cities we explored. The whitewashed waterfront homes with the colorful roofs, door frames, and shutters proved to be the highlights of our short stay, ultimately ending in me taking away Manny's iPod for a few hours after catching him taking too many pictures instead of soaking up the experience with the lenses of his own eyes. The photos we took of each other on the cliffs overlooking the crystal-clear water below now hang in the newly painted and redesigned living room, all of which had Manny striking cliché poses that thousands of visitors did every single day.

Our last leg to Santorini was somewhat disappointingly uneventful, seeing as how it was geared more for young couples and time spent laying outside in the sun as opposed to visiting historical locations and ancient structures. It was remarkably similar to Mykonos in a geographical and visual sense, with captivating architecture that complimented the ocean around it all. Alleys could barely fit two people, tourist attractions were surprisingly hard to come by, and family-owned restaurants and stores were fairly difficult to find. Although it didn't quite live up to Athens or Mykonos, Santorini still stole our hearts much like the other two parts of our adventure in its own unique way. Ranking our favorite moments on the flight home, we were both in agreement that the nighttime dinner at a small outdoor café on the coast of Mykonos was singlehandedly the most incredible part of our trip. We sat gaping at all of the lights, strung over our heads and reflecting on the water all around us. The perfect medium between the nightlife and the live music was that it was just quiet enough for us to be able to hear the gentle splash of the waves hitting the rocks below us. Neither one of us could give it justice even if we tried!

Returning home was bittersweet, but much needed. Manny was anxious to get back into physical therapy and testing out his arm, whereas I had to reacclimate myself to my classes and catch up on all of my missed marketing work at the firm during the time we were gone. It was time for the two of us to fall back into our routine, but we made a promise to each other before we got out of the truck in the wee hours of the morning after returning that Saturday. The two of us, father and son, were going to finish off Emma's bucket list before the end of the summer. Manny had just under four weeks left until he had to head back to school, but he was confident that we would be able to check off the final eight objectives in no time. "I think we both need to do this, Papa," he said sleepily before unlocking his truck door. "I'm ready if you are." With pride searing through my veins and a tear in my eye, my mind flashed back to the evening on the Chesapeake, and for a second it was as if Emmy were in the truck with me instead of Manny. "I've never felt so ready to make this thing finally happen. I've been waiting for this since I was a little older than you are now. Let's write this final chapter, for her. Sound like a plan?"

Lifting his suitcase out of the truck bed, he looked up at me, his perfectly green eyes somehow still shining in the darkness as we stood in the driveway. He winked. "Demand a happy ending, Papa." I waited for him to carry his things inside before reaching into my back pocket and taking out my tear-soaked letter from Emma. Reading it out loud to myself in the dim light of the moon, I repeated, "Thank you for breaking down the walls that I desperately refused to put down. And most importantly, thank you for giving us a chance. It's beautiful, the depth of our love being surmised by a simple word like 'Always.' It isn't just a word; it's a promise that there will always be a sense of love between the two of us. I love you and I always will. Yours, Emma"

Two soft tears rolled down my cheeks, smearing the ink only oh so slightly in the light of my garage door flood lights. She would have been so proud of the young man he was slowly becoming. This was now Manny's

story too, and I knew then that I was ready to help him write it.

1) Go Christmas Caroling in the Summer

2) Get Matching Tattoos

3) Steal Free Samples

4) Star Gaze from a Truck Bed

5) Test Drive a Sports Car

6) Follow Jogger While Blaring "Eye of the Tiger"

7) Point Hair Dryer Out Car Window (Fake Radar Gun)

8) Be in Two States at Once

Letting out an exhaustive sigh, I read aloud the last eight checkpoints

on Emma's bucket list, sitting in disbelief as to how someone so wickedly

intelligent could come up with such a goofy list of things to do. I mean,

really, caroling in the summer? "Hey, at least all of this stuff can be done in

the next four weeks. There aren't any events listed here that are specific to

spring, winter, or fall, so that helps," said Manny, reassuringly. So, there we

sat, pushing aside our empty bowls of cereal (almost all that we could afford after the Greece trip) so that we could look at the remainder of the list and plan out how and when we were going to make all of this work. Between catching up on my classes and getting in hours at work, we'd have approximately four full weekends to cross off the majority of the remaining feats.

Manny pulled out a calendar and a pencil from one of the drawers in the kitchen. "How about we go caroling this Tuesday, just to get it over with?" He stopped no less than three or four times to giggle while trying to get that sentence out. "Why this Tuesday?" "Because I remember hearing you mention something about an exam on Wednesday and I figure maybe you can get rid of all the nerves. Who knows? Maybe singing unseasonal tunes to a bunch of strangers on their front porches will work wonders for you." His sarcasm was sharp enough to cut through steel. "Your rationale sucks, but fine. Tuesday it is," I said. Scribbling it into the calendar, we went through the other seven activities that we needed to accomplish, assigning them to different days from then through the end of August, just before Manny had to go back to school. Penciling in two dates per week may have seemed a tad hectic, but we knew without a shred of doubt that we'd be able to make it work. Falling short wasn't an option.

We decided to wait until Tuesday evening to gear up in our red and green, put on our Santa hats, and walk around the outermost edge of our neighborhood, knocking on doors and belting out "Jingle Bells," "Rudolph the Red-Nosed Reindeer," and "Silent Night." By then, people would be home from work and have their feet kicked up on the coffee table, enjoying whatever show was on around primetime that evening. "There's no way that I'm doing this for any longer than an hour," barked Manny, wiping the sweat off his eyebrows with his thick, itchy Christmas sweater. "I told you three times to just wear a green t-shirt! But, what do I know?" "I wanted to play the part, but I didn't think it would be this humid." "Really? It's the beginning of August, and you expect it not to be humid?" Nudging me just enough to knock me off the sidewalk, Manny smirked at my sense of sarcasm, knowing right away that he had it coming to him.

We scoped out a large Victorian style home with a few lights turned on inside and a bright red front door. Sighing and looking at one another, we walked up the porch steps and stood about a foot apart. "Want to just do Jingle Bells and then get out of here?" he asked. "Yeah," I whispered back, just before lifting my right fist and making three solid knocks on the door. About ten seconds later, a middle-aged lady appeared from behind the door, first looking at me, then looking down at Manny, visibly confused. Glancing over at him, I slowly opened my mouth and started singing off of our printed-off carol sheet, making sure that we didn't botch the lyrics or notes. Halfway through the song, I lifted my gaze up to the woman, only to see that her husband (a tall, burly looking fellow) had joined her in watching us sing, both of whom had a smile on their face. I had to fight back a smile because this is exactly what Emmy would have wanted. Our two-man duet wrapped up only a minute or two later, leading us into an awkward silence as the couple stood, waiting to see if we had any other tunes up our sleeves. "Well done!" she proclaimed, her smile revealing an almost perfectly white set of teeth.

Coming to the conclusion that we were done, she slowed down her initially lightning-quick clap of her hands, the husband following suit. I bowed—don't worry, it really wasn't all that awkward—and thanked them for their time. Manny also thanked them for listening, and we turned around, hurriedly making our way down to the sidewalk, both wanting to hit full stride and run away from the couple that was still watching us from the top step outside of their home. "Dude, that may have easily been the silliest five minutes of my entire life," Manny said jokingly. "Right? It was fun though, seeing their reaction once they swung the door open." We reluctantly targeted another five or six houses (only three of them answered), bringing laughs and smiles to them all, telling them that "Santa was only five months away" and to have a "very merry summer."

Soaked through our clothes, we navigated our way back home, all the while chatting about how embarrassed we both felt, but relieved at the fact that it was over with. Manny took the liberty upon himself to take a pen through that line on the list, already talking about how much fun test driving a sports car would be. I wasn't entirely sure where or how I was going to make it happen, but fortunately, I still had another three days to decide. Oh, Emma, if you only knew the half of it.

"The dealership is literally right there, why are you pulling in here?" Cutting my turn to the left, I pulled into the parking lot just outside of a small convenience store, directly across the street from the only Audi dealership in our area. "What are they going to think when I pull up in something that looks like this, asking them to get behind the wheel of an R8?" I kicked the truck with the heel of my shoe, almost expecting my foot to go the whole way through the rusted metal. Manny sported a pair of khakis and a button-down shirt and I was in my favorite charcoal colored suit with a light purple necktie. We knew that in order to pull this off, there couldn't be any loose ends—we needed to play the part. Pushing open the showroom door, we were confronted instantaneously by a short, muscularly-built gentleman in a polo shirt with "Audi" stitched onto the front.

"Cal," he said as he extended his hand. Grasping it firmly with my own, I replied "Liam. This is my son, Manny." Manny smiled warmly as he shook the salesman's hand also. "What brings you in this evening? You two look awfully sharp, by the way!" His enthusiasm was already playing out the way I had been hoping in my mind. I chuckled, trying to give off a slightly reserved, yet professional sort of swagger. "I've been intrigued by what I've been reading about the new RS7s. They put out close to 450 horse power now, correct?" Manny looked up at me, impressed at how smoothly I was playing this game of cards. "Oh, sir, right this way." Following Cal's lead, I whispered to Manny, "Just because I drive a piece of crap doesn't mean I'm uncultured when it comes to this stuff. And by the way, this bucket list idea was all mine." I gave him a wink. Our short walk across the showroom floor lead us to a brand new, jet black Audi RS7. Casually, I opened the driver's side door and slid in, needing to adjust the seat for my tall, lean stature. Rambling off some random things I knew about the model (like the cruise control, added sensors, and increased torque), I meticulously inspected the interior, slowly but surely reeling Cal into my imaginary net, ready to scoop him up and drop him into an ice-filled cooler.

"Eh, it's sporty, but not particularly my thing. I was expecting something a little edgier. I just got rid of my Continental to help put another few bucks into the remodeling of our house down at the shore, and if his mom knew we were already looking at something else, she'd kill us both." His eyebrows perked up, automatically recognizing my Bentley reference and soaring his impression of our social class through the roof of that showroom. "May I ask what exactly you're hoping to find, now that it seems you don't see an RS7 in your garage anytime soon?" He looked nervous, unsure as to whether he had anything more to say that would keep our interest in him and his lineup of cars. "We have the A8, the S7, the—" Manny cut him off. "We want to see the R8." The offhand comment turned both my head and Cal's, spinning around to see Manny running his fingers across the hood of the R8, one of the nastiest beasts in the world of exotic sports cars.

Holding back my sudden urge to laugh at how perfectly this was panning out, I strode over to the vehicle with my hands comfortably in my pockets. I made two or three circles around the car, occasionally crouching down to look at the design of a tire spoke or quietly reading the paperwork attached to its door handle aloud to myself. Cal stood behind me, watching intently, as he knew that the R8 was in a league all on its own. Doing as I did several minutes before, I crawled into the 610-horsepower machine and let my guard down, the inner kid within me rose to life, and I smiled from ear to ear. By then, Cal had made his way over to the open car door, grinning in reaction to the sheer joy I was feeling. "Jesus, this is unreal." "You wouldn't believe the number of people that come in here, just to ask if they could get a picture inside of it." "Yeah, I can only imagine. What's this thing run, $150,000? $175,000?" I could tell it was used and I knew that it was a bit of an older model, so I decided to overestimate its face value so I could coax him into thinking that whatever he was pricing it at was well within the bounds of my imaginary income. The fact that it was a used car significantly helped out our odds in getting some time out on the road, but the sun was descending rapidly, and I wasn't about to drive it any other time than in the daylight.

"Well, this is actually a trade-in that we just got a week or two ago from some financial consultant a county or two over. He took what we gave him, went out, and supposedly used it to put a down payment on a brand-new yacht in the Inner Harbor. Insane." Still waiting to hear a figure, I kept looking at him until he realized that he hadn't yet answered my question. "Right now, you're looking at around $90,000 because of the mileage. It's just above 45,000 miles, and that's part of the reason it's been a tough sale to make. Not many people want a car that pricey, especially one that has that many miles under the hood." "Hey, that's not a bad deal if you ask me." Flabbergasted, Manny totally lost sight of how we were supposed to be in character and looked at me like I was crazy. Compared to the lifestyle the two of us lived, he was absolutely right. "What's the likelihood that I'd be allowed to get a few minutes on the road with this thing?" Hesitant, Cal said that they hadn't yet allowed anyone to do so. "Well, you also said that you haven't had any legitimate customers over the past two weeks, didn't you?" "I guess you're right. Let me talk to my manager," Cal said just before disappearing behind a door that apparently led to the dealership's offices. I reached over the shifter to Manny who was sitting in the passenger seat and gave him a fist bump as my sly grin grew even larger.

He emerged a few moments later, gripping two sets of keys. My heart stopped. "Here are three forms I'll need you to fill out. I need to see your ID and proof of insurance. Your signature is required here, here, and here." Handing him my information, I took the pen and scratchily wrote my name where he had initially pointed to. Meanwhile, he was opening the large glass showroom door so that we would be able to pull out and into the parking lot. It had gone entirely over my head that it was only a two-seater, which meant that only one of us (Manny or myself) would be able to experience it at a time. Sticking the keys into the ignition, the engine roared to life, sending waves of pure adrenaline from my feet down near the gas pedal, up my legs, and eventually up my spine to the point where all of my hair stood on end. My death grip on the steering wheel relaxed, but my heart was still racing. Cal, riding shotgun, instructed me on all of the power and shift functions in the car as we made our way out of the parking lot and up the block. I accelerated onto the highway's onramp, making Cal nervous enough to ask me to keep things safe. It wasn't that fast, I promise.

We popped off the interstate and made one giant circle back to the dealership where I got out, swapping places with Cal and ushering Manny into the passenger seat so he could see what it felt like to ride in such a luxury car. Evidently, Cal wanted to show off, because as soon as he had some open room, he floored it out of the parking lot and down the two-lane road out in front of the dealership, giving anyone around us a taste of what a revved-up supercar sounds like. They returned a few minutes later, Manny emerging with an enormous smile on his face. "Mr. Cal, thank you so much. Since my mom doesn't listen to my dad too often, I promise to put in a good word as soon as we get home!" I smacked my hand to my forehead—what a suck-up! I helped Cal back the R8 into its original spot on the showroom floor and helped him lock the glass door back into place. "I'd be lying if I said that this thing doesn't live up to the Continental and then some." "Well, once you talk things over with the Mrs., we would love to touch base with you about moving forward with the paperwork." "I have a feeling we'll be on the same page," I said smiling, knowing that Emma was looking down at Manny and me, shaking her head in embarrassment.

I took Cal's business card, thanked him for his time, and began walking across the street to the sad reality that was my truck. Just before stepping in, I looked back at the showroom to make sure he hadn't watched us leave. Thankfully, he was polishing up the R8, making it look as clean as possible for the next pair of father-son jokesters to walk in the door. "Six more to go! That was so much fun." "Yeah, buddy, it sure was." He looked

up at me and smiled before asking, "You know what that salesman said

when we were on our drive?" "What's that?" "You must have one awesome

mom to let you and your dad look at getting a car like this one." I paused,

waiting to hear what else Manny had to say. After a few seconds, he said "I

agreed with him." I smiled, putting my hand on his shoulder. "She's with us,

just looking after us both from a different place, buddy." "Yeah, I know she

is, Papa."

The anxiety of summer classes was nearing its end, with my final

exams falling in line with the six remaining bucket list checkpoints that

Manny and I were scheduled to finish. Never in a million years had I

expected any of this to happen: tackling depression and alcoholism,

rediscovering the presence of God, becoming a father, and finishing the list

that Emma and I vowed to complete all of those years ago. The next feat to

be reached was matching tattoos, something I was yet to wrap my mind

around. I got in contact with the guy who owned a tattoo shop about five

minutes from our house and scheduled a time to go in, only a few hours after the first of my final exams; I was ecstatic to be in the homestretch of my classes and so was Manny. When we first walked in the door, we were both taken aback by some of the eerie pieces of artwork that we saw on the walls, but we felt relieved to see a man in his latter twenties appear and introduce himself before taking us into the back room.

In the days prior, we both decided that we'd honor Emma by using her word, 'Always,' and incorporating baseball, something that the two of us had bonded over since Manny was a little boy. No, I was not about to let him get a legitimate tattoo just yet, so his would be one of those fake tattoos that disappears in a few weeks—you know, the press-on kind. Drawing up a quick design before the actual process began, he made a rough draft that had 'Always' laced together in cursive, but in red baseball seams. I was scared because of the sloppy nature of the draft (and the fact that I didn't know what to expect pain-wise), but he assured me that it would look entirely different once it was finished and that I needed to trust him. No big deal, just a piece of art that will be on my body, more specifically my back shoulder, for the rest of my life. Seriously, I was sweating bullets.

The sound of the machine sent somewhat of a shiver down my spine, my anxiety reaching a climax as I sensed the presence of the needle, only milliseconds before hitting my skin. Manny's awestruck face was hilarious. I guess he was in disbelief that I was actually getting a tattoo. The needle's jabs were freakishly fast and it felt like someone was writing on my sunburnt shoulder blade with a sharp pencil. Wincing at first, I didn't expect the pain to subside so soon. It was only a minute or two in when my skin finally grew numb, leaving the pain much less severe and entirely bearable. The tattoo artist began asking about the significance of the design, so I told him everything from the bucket list to Emma and Manny. At one point, he had to take a second to wipe away tears, sharing with us that he too lost his mom from the ravages of breast cancer only a year prior. It hit me, as it has the unsung tendency of doing, just how far of a reach that cancer has across everyone and everything. I told him that Emmy's battle had given us so much more than it had taken away and that his mom was in a much better place, watching over him, hoping his heart was no longer heavy.

An hour passed, the skin on my shoulder feeling more irritated every minute. My eyes closed and I felt the dull pain of the needle disappear. I heard the machine turn off, just before a cold wipe came sliding across my scapula. "Ready to check it out?" I had been watching Manny's facial expression out of the corner of my eye ever since we started, but he was so focused that I had a hard time gauging whether he was impressed or horrified by how it looked. Spinning around to catch a glimpse in the dual-mirror, my jaw dropped at the raw talent covering my back shoulder. The color and the lines, the shading, and the cursive letters were unlike anything on his sketch pad. The baseball seams were almost three-dimensional looking, able to trick a stranger into thinking they were actual laces going in and out of my body. Manny walked over to us from his seat in the corner, gently tracing over the elevated skin with a smile on his face. A clear, odorless liquid was sprayed across my back to help the ink settle into the skin properly. I was told explicitly not to scratch any itches in that general area, not to go swimming for any extended periods of time for the next few weeks, and to apply sunscreen regularly if I found myself outside and shirtless, so as to protect and maintain the integrity of the red color.

Manny plopped down in the chair, staring intently as the guy replicated my tattoo, which was already beginning to itch like crazy, with some special paint on a fiber-like material. Wetting Manny's arm, he applied the freshly painted design onto his skin, holding it tightly for several minutes to allow it to stick to his skin. Peeling off the sheet of paper left Manny thrilled, feeling so badass at the fact that he'd be able to show it off to his classmates in the coming weeks, savoring its intricacy before it faded away in another month's time. Thanking the man, I pulled out my wallet to pay him for his time and service, again reminding him that his mom was no longer suffering and in a much better place. I was baffled when he reached out and closed the open wallet in my hands, pushing it away in the direction of the back pocket I just took it out from. "I don't need that. You've already given me enough today. I think it's amazing what you two are doing. I'm expecting my first boy in another few months, and hearing what you guys have been through and how you're embracing it is a lesson I couldn't ever afford to pay for. Take that money and give it to the cancer center or something, in honor of my mom. Her name was Alonza. Alonza Robinson."

I tucked the money away into my wallet, putting it back into my pocket. Stepping forward, I embraced the young man in a tight hug. Manny wrapped his arms around us too. Somewhere up above the clouds, I was positive that Emmy and Ms. Robinson were together, relishing in that moment the same way the three of us were. God's magic was alive and well in that tattoo parlor. The swelling on my back shoulder didn't compare to the swelling within my heart. On the way home, I pulled up in front of the cancer treatment wing of the hospital and Manny hopped out of the truck, ran inside with the money, and came back out nearly ten minutes later with a smile that somehow managed not to show his teeth. "They had a donation box and little cards to write on, so I wrote down *In Memory of Alonza R.* and dropped it in with the money. All good?" "All good."

3.60. A 3.60 GPA! An A in Human Anatomy, an A- in Basic Nutrition, an A in Physiology, a B+ in Nursing Science, and a B in Human Development, plus a handful of other credits from online modules and certifications. What was easily the most agonizing summer workload I'd ever had to deal with had finally reached its end, sending me into the last two weeks of Manny's summer vacation with five more bucket list items left. Manny and I drove into the city for an Orioles game to celebrate the conclusion of my summer-long program. Scarfing down two disgustingly-loaded chili cheese dogs from a food cart outside the stadium, we walked down Eutaw Street and through the outfield gates. We broke into the bank account yet again, which made me pray even more that Manny could get a full-ride academic and athletic scholarship somewhere after he graduated from high school in another couple of years.

I purchased two seats about four rows behind the Orioles dugout, a handsome reward for a grueling summer of stress and chaotic class schedules. It was a Friday night game against the Yankees, so there wasn't an open seat in the whole place. The legion of orange colored shirts was plagued with small bands of navy blue as if they were infiltrating enemy forces. Six home runs and a stellar pitching performance by our bullpen were enough to hold off New York for an 8-5 victory, capping off a phenomenal week of final exams.

Later that next week, Manny and I debated for a while about the order of our final five events. Although my classes were finally over, I still had to put in a decent number of hours at the real estate firm, doing the same old marketing work that I'd been doing for years. Sitting at just under fourteen days until Manny would be back in class, gearing up for his last year of middle school, we found ourselves looking blankly at the closing lines of the August calendar. He wanted desperately to steal free samples, but I thought the way I had planned it all out in my head was much, much better. "Why can't we combine the fake radar gun prank and motivating the joggers? It'll save us a day to do them both at once, which would only leave us with being in two states at once, truck bed star-gazing, and stealing free samples to finish this thing once and for all." "How about Monday before you have to go to work, we skip our morning run and go to Powell Park? I know there's a ton of people who walk their dogs and jog there every morning. Then we can do the hair dryer radar gun thing before we go home and so you can get ready to head into the office." Before I even answered his proposal, he was already erasing and rewriting our plan on the calendar for the beginning of next week. "That works for me," I said as I held the list in my hands, admiring how perfect of a line the spaghetti sauce had dried into.

The half-blown-out subwoofer in the back seat of my tattered truck pulsated as Survivor's "Eye of the Tiger" roared to life (pun intended) and blared out of the stereo in the dashboard. Humidity from outside our open windows rolled into the front seat, mixing with the cold air from the air conditioning unit, leaving myself and a sleepy Manny quite comfortable, sitting patiently in the lot beside Powell Park just before 6:00 a.m. We (well, mostly me because Manny's eyes were half-closed) were scoping out the other side of the park where the sidewalk comes around the corner and runs parallel to the road. I wasn't entirely sure why the song was already playing, but I belted out the lyrics, trying my hardest to wake up the slug in my passenger seat.

In the distance, I could barely make out the image of a man jogging down the long straight-away in the center of the park by the car path. Knowing that our time was of the essence, I smacked Manny on the back of the head and yelled, "It's show time!" as loud as I possibly could. He jolted, visibly annoyed by my uncalled-for exuberance. "I'm never going to get a job that makes me wake up this early to go to work every day. No chance." At his age, I was saying the same exact thing. Heck, I was still saying the same thing back then, too. I threw it into reverse and spun out of the lot, creeping up slowly behind the runner like a lion stalking a gazelle. I allowed Manny to do the honors, taking the volume dial and cranking it up slowly as we grew closer. Thirty feet. Twenty feet. Fifteen feet. Ten feet. Five feet. All of a sudden, just as the main chorus of the song was about to begin, Manny took the volume as high as it would go. The runner immediately spun around, frightened by the thundering music.

Manny and I each pulled out our pairs of cheap plastic sunglasses, even though the sun wasn't even in the sky at that point, and stared at the man, his strides beginning to widen, our truck continuing to speed up. Our heads bopped up and down to the rhythmic thud of the bass, our eyes still glued to the runner. Once the runner realized what exactly we were doing, his expression of horror turned into one of humor as he started to chuckle at our pitiful attempt at being funny and cheering him on. He came to a stop, catching his breath in-between his hysterical fits of laughter. Not being able to control ourselves either, Manny and I busted into stitches, dumbfounded at how much funnier this was in real life as opposed to a bullet point on paper. We rolled on, grinning as the runner waved to us in the rearview mirror, a smile still on his face as he bent down to retie his shoes. We made a U-turn and headed back to our spot in the parking lot, awaiting our next victim.

About an hour and a half passed, leaving us with only four more runners, two of which heard a car with blaring music behind them and ran off the sidewalk and into the grassy center of the field, scared at who might be creeping up behind them. Yes, Manny and I felt plenty guilty about scaring them off, but they never gave us a chance to show them what we were trying to do. Well, at least that's what we told ourselves. As for the other two, an older couple, they smiled at our cheesiness and gave us two thumbs up for our creativity. The woman yelled out, "If I could go any faster, I would!" as we sped ahead, making a beeline down a nearby backroad that was notorious for speeding tickets, especially on the way to work every morning.

Pulling off the side of the road, just over the crest of the hill, so we were out of sight for any speeding cars, I turned off the truck and reached into the back seat, pulling out an old hair dryer that had once belonged to Emmy. I still had a lot of her things, things that I knew I couldn't just give away or throw in the trash. I held onto the hair dryer because I loved waking up and walking into our bathroom, seeing her crank it up to full power and send her hair flying back behind her neck in a wave of heat. I held onto that hair dryer because even when she lost her hair, she kept it plugged in on the vanity like she refused to lose sight of a day when it'd grow back. Emma was the type of person who'd rather die trying than to give up. She fought back with guns blazing until she ran out of ammo. It was one of the millions of reasons I loved her as much as what I did.

I rolled down the window and stuck the hairdryer out just far enough that it was visible next to my side mirror. It couldn't have been any more than a minute after we got there that a small Nissan coupe came flying down over the top of the hill. With our truck position about thirty yards down from the top, there would be no way for someone to slow down enough to meet the 35-mph speed limit before passing our "unmarked" vehicle. The Nissan's brake pads had to have turned to dust—okay, maybe I'm being a little bit dramatic, but it was close. Their brake lights lit up instantly as they slowed down, probably ten miles per hour under the speed limit. If I were actually a police officer, it wouldn't have helped their cause. We sat, Manny and I, in the front seat, laughing hysterically at how these reckless speedsters continued to fall for our stupid prop. I grew increasingly nervous that a cop would come up over the top of the hill, see what I was doing, and haul me off to the slammer for impersonating law enforcement. The two of us had our laughs and decided enough was enough, using the old pen from the glove box to, yet again, make our list even shorter.

"I wonder how much jail time you'd get for impersonating a cop." "Hey, this wasn't my idea. You have Emma to thank; she's probably peeing herself laughing at how stupid we look doing all of these things." "I don't know how she even came up with this stuff. I mean seriously, a blow dryer as a radar gun?" "Don't get me started," I said. "Did I ever tell you about the time she chopped off all of my hair?" The look on his face was priceless.

✝

"This is so much less climactic than it seemed on paper," I said. "Was this supposed to be fun?" asked Manny. "Just take it in, give it another five minutes and we'll leave." "Papa, there's a rock that's pinching my ass." "Did you really have to swear?" "Okay, sorry." Cars flew by us, cruising anywhere between 60 and 80 miles per hour, shooting pebbles in our direction and leaving gusts of draft rustling our hair. Hazard lights flashed on the back of the truck as we lay on our backs, staring at the sky from the shoulder of I83 N. The little sign reading "Mason Dixon Line" was stuck in the ground at an odd angle, directly to our right. The sun was going down, marking the end of the second-to-last Friday of Manny's summer before his eighth-grade school year was set to begin. Any other time, I'd say that driving the whole way to another state just for the heck of it, then turning around and going home would be the biggest waste of time and gas. But, since it was for the sake of getting the list completed, it was well worth it. "How does it feel?" "How does what feel?" "Being able to scratch your head in Maryland and cross your legs in Pennsylvania at the same time." Sarcastically, Manny lifted his hand to his head and began to scratch while his legs crossed over each other. We both laughed, thinking about what the people driving by were thinking when they saw a man and a boy lying flat on their backs beside a major highway.

"Okay, I can't take this anymore." Manny angrily picked himself up off the ground and bent down to retrieve the pesky piece of asphalt that had brought him so much irritation over the past couple of minutes. He took two steps back and launched it into the neighboring cornfield. "I literally just threw something the whole way from Maryland to Pennsylvania." "You're an idiot, have I ever told you that?" I said, trying not to laugh. "I don't want to hear it. I get it from you!" I stood up, chasing after him as he ducked into the car, hitting the lock button so I couldn't get in to antagonize him. Every day we grew more and more like best friends, always forgetting that we were older than the age we acted. Throwing up my figurative white flag, I earned his trust and jumped back into the driver's seat, pulling away from the side of the road and hopping off the next exit before turning around to drive home.

The sun was sinking rapidly below the edge of the surrounding pastures and neighborhoods, the stars slowly making their way into the blanket of the moonlight. I remember thinking to myself just how perfectly clear that night was, frustrating me that I had to focus on the road instead of peering out the window, taking in the deep red hue of the already vanished sun. "Hey," I said, snapping Manny out of his trance looking out at the night sky. "Why not do another double-up? You know, cross two things off the list in one day. Look outside, you can't possibly tell me that you think there will be another night over the next week that's as nice as this one." I rolled down the window, letting a warm rush of air persuade Manny's decision to mark off "truck bed stargazing" from the list. Taking another look out the window just as he had done only a couple of seconds prior, he smiled. "We'd be down to one last checkpoint. Let's do this." I think the excitement we both felt was at an all-time high. The hidden treasure that Manny stumbled upon, which was left dormant in my nightstand for so many years, was nearing its completion at a rapid pace.

Through her humor, creativity, and beauty, Emma gave my son and I the chance to grow connected in a way that no one else had ever done before. She led us overseas, made us laugh until our ribs hurt, and cry until our noses ran. Emma's list was much more than a list; it was a promise of adventure and a way for Manny and me to rediscover ourselves and what we both loved above all else—each other. Emmy was a guardian angel to us both, bringing Manny out of a life without a family and thrusting him into my pit of despair. We were unbreakable, undeniably lost in the best friendship either one of us had ever experienced—even more so than what I had with Em. Through her, we both were given a second chance at life. Through each other, we gave Emma the storybook ending she deserved.

After much deliberation, we decided that Powell Park was probably the most logical spot to camp out and allow our eyes to wander across hundreds of trillions of miles into the unexplored universe. I pulled up out in front of our house and shifted the truck into park as Manny ran in to grab an armful of blankets and pillows that he then tossed into the truck bed. Pulling into a grassy opening in the park's center, we didn't have a single tree blocking our view, a single car distracting us from enjoying our moment, nor any sign of life to bother us other than the chirp of thousands of crickets in the woods off to our right. I stepped up onto the tailgate and helped Manny climb in, rearranging all of the pillows and blankets to make one giant, comfortable pit of soft plush. I reclined, resting my head on the very back of the truck bed, bringing a blanket up to cover my body and keep me away from the chilly breeze of the August night.

Manny's arms were wrapped around his bent knees, a smaller blanket wrapped around his shoulders. We didn't even talk for what seemed like forever, the two of us allowing ourselves to be swallowed up by the darkness around us, illuminated by only the light of the moon. I broke the silence by reaching my arm over and placing my hand on Manny's shoulder. "I know that I've said it before and that you've probably grown tired of hearing me say it, but I will never be able to tell you how much I love you and how proud I am of you. The greatest blessing in my life has been merging our lives together and raising the greatest young man I've ever met." Manny's eyes glistened in the moonlight when he turned his head to me, his warm smile bringing a tear to my eye, reminding me just how blessed I was to have him in my life. "You're going to grow up to be ungodly successful, son, more so than I could have ever dreamt of being. You're going to fall in love, grow old with somebody, and you're going to be their world—just like you are mine. And I promise you, there will never, ever be a day when you can't come to me and talk about something. I don't care whether you're scared of upsetting me or what consequences there may be, I'll be here for you."

Reaching across my body with my left arm, I gave a subtle tap on my back-right shoulder where my new tattoo had finally begun setting in, hinting at 'Always'. "I want to be half the dad you've been to me, Papa.

Even just half, because then I'd know that I'm doing something right. And I want to find someone who cares about me the same way you care about Emma, even now that she's gone. I know she's in a better place, but you make it seem like she hasn't even left. Sometimes I feel like she's with us when we're doing these things. I don't know how to explain it, but it does." A wide grin spread across my face, relating exactly to Manny's words and what he claimed to feel. Emma was one of those stars, likely the brightest one up there, blushing at the sincerity of Manny's words and wishing that she was there to give him one of her characteristically tight hugs.

I blurted out, "Can you believe that it boils down to one more line? This time tomorrow, the list can be finished, the final page can be flipped." "It's been a lot of fun, Papa." Looking away from the beautiful starry projection, I scooted over to Manny, giving him a one-armed hug. I thought to myself, what if one day Manny makes a list with his own wife? Or his own kid? The thought of one day being a grandfather was surreal to me, finding it hard to consider that I'd ever be able to love another little boy or girl the way I loved my own. It was my own little wrinkle in time, a mere speck underneath the entirety of God's creation that engulfed our truck, the park, and the rest of our world. I closed my eyes and accepted the chilling gusts of wind that nipped at my ears. I focused on the melody of the crickets, marching in tune together by the thousands. I felt Manny's short breaths as he placed his head on my shoulder, exhausted from yet another lengthy day. Everything I needed in the world was right there with me in the back of my truck. I felt God's grace. I felt Emma's love. But most of all, I felt excitement for what was the end of a remarkable adventure, less than a day away. I let my thoughts drift off, sensing Manny's slumber already in the works. By the time we both woke up, it was only a matter of hours until Emmy's list would appear to be nothing more than a boat registration with thick, crossed out lines littered across the front and back. The beautiful thing was that it was so, so much more.

We rode in complete silence, well aware of how much time, effort, blood, sweat, and tears led us up to the moments just ahead of us. I could tell how emotional of an experience this was going to be for Manny, almost like a funeral for the last living piece of the mother he should have had. My emotions were surging, confused as to whether I should be thrilled about the imminent completion of Emmy's beloved bucket list, or heartbroken at the fact that she wasn't there to take part in it with us. It was early in the afternoon, the sun was high in the sky, and our truck screeched to a halt in the fourth parking space out in front of an old shopping mart. Looking through the store window, I could see shoppers pushing their rusted yellow grocery carts down one aisle, then popping a turn and repeating the process all over again. I let out a deep sigh, taking Manny's hand into my own. "Can I tell you something?" I asked. "Yeah." "This was where Emma and I crossed off our first activity from the list." He turned, revealing two watery eyes. "We were just a little bit older than you are now. We came here and scouted the aisles, commentating every move that the shoppers would make like they were in the Olympics. Trust me, it was hilarious." He smirked, shaking his head in pure embarrassment.

God's plan never ceased to amaze me, bringing life back around to special places and special people. There I sat, with the newfound love of my life, my son, staring down the store where this whole adventure began. Stepping out of the truck, we embraced each other one last time before stepping through the automatic door and into the store. Per the store's website, they had regularly scheduled sample stands set up every Saturday, aligning perfectly with the calendar that Manny and I had mapped out.

Scanning the aisles, reminiscing on my trip here with Emma, I spotted a pitifully constructed cardboard display with little circular cups filled with what appeared to be ice cream. There were approximately ten to fifteen cups scattered across the droopy cardboard stand, manned by a teenage girl who was chewing gum sloppily and sneaking looks down at her phone that was out of sight. She looked only a few years older than Manny, which I was determined to have play to our advantage. I tugged on his shirt, encouraging him to follow me into the adjacent aisle to devise our heist.

"So, this is how it's going to work—you're going to go ask her where the sunflower seeds are. When she tells you, come straight back here. We'll give it a minute and then send you back so you can ask her to take you there because you 'still can't seem to find it.'" He chuckled at my air quotes. "As soon as you two leave the stand, I'm going to make a run for it and grab all of the cups, so meet me in Aisle 1. Deal?" "Deal." He gave me a fist bump, spinning himself around and puffing out his chest, entirely focused on making this the best accomplishment yet. I peeked around the side of the shelving, only to see him chatting with her and pointing in the direction of where his favorite snack was supposed to be found. Walking unsuspectingly back to where I was standing, he gave me two thumbs up. We counted out loud until we reached sixty, sending him back for the final leg of the mission, bringing us only seconds away from our greatest achievement as father and son.

Returning to the stand, Manny shrugged his shoulders and again pointed in the general vicinity of the seeds. The girl smiled warmly, leading the way down the aisle and around the corner, passing me by only feet away. My entire body began to warm up, starting in my toes as I began to take long strides towards the stand of free samples. My stomach felt like a butterfly sanctuary and the hair on the back of my neck stood on end. In only a couple of seconds, I arrived at the table, turning in every direction to make sure no one else was watching me in the act. The coast was clear, and I started cramming cups of vanilla bean ice cream into my pockets, making room in my cradled arms for the rest of the samples. The stack of ice cream cups exceeded the space in my hands and arms, towering up close to my eyes. I shuffled my feet in a way that allowed me to move quickly without tripping and spilling my lactic treasure all over the floor. Popping a left-hand turn, I cut into a small enclave of empty cardboard boxes by the swinging doors in the back of the store.

I watched as the girl made her way back to the subpar display, scratching her head and looking all around to see how the dozen cups were all taken by customers in such a short span of her absence, or if somehow, they were merely misplaced. Manny (who was holding two bags of barbeque flavored sunflower seeds) strolled around the edge of the aisle directly ahead of me, spotting me almost immediately. Hitting full sprint, he tossed the two bags into an open space on the adjacent shelving unit and carried his momentum all the way over to me. In all of my years of being a father and a best friend to Manny, I hadn't ever seen him so emotionally charged. It was as if I had just returned from war, the same reaction taking place when he jumped into my arms. He sent four cups toppling to the floor, yelling "We did it! We did it!" just loud enough to turn the head of a shopper rolling by in his electric cart. He snatched three of the cups out my hands, using his middle and index fingers as a make-shift spoon, scooping out the milky dessert.

Missing his face completely, the vanilla bean frozen treat dripped from the corner of his mouth and down his shirt. "Yes, buddy, we did." I too used my fingers as a utensil to get the ice cream out of the remaining cups, tossing the empty plastic cups into one of the empty boxes over my shoulder.

A lone tear streaming down the right side of my face, I whispered, "Always," into Manny's ear. He withdrew the list from his back pocket, held tightly at its fold by the clip of a ballpoint pen. He clicked open the pen, kneeling down and positioning the piece of paper on the cardboard flap of a potato chip box. It took every fiber of my being not to cry, watching him move his hand back and forth, leaving the final line of the list scribbled out in an inky mess. He took a moment, looking down from the top of the page, flipping it over onto its other side to absorb just how many feats were reached both during and after Emma's time on Earth. With two hands, gripping the registration pamphlet as if it were made of glass, Manny placed the bucket list in my open palms, treating it like a sacred document. For being a loud mouth, I was speechless, simply looking down at the magic in-between my fingers, overcome by my loss for words. "We did it. We did it." The floodgates behind my eyeballs gave way, and a rush of tears escaped and poured down my cheeks, making Manny follow suit.

In the wildest turn of events, our adventure had reached its conclusion inside a cave of boxes at the tail-end of a shopping mart. From the shores of Mykonos to a tattoo parlor, the bed of a truck in the middle of the night to the front porches of dozens of strangers with sheets of Christmas hits in our hands, we had reached the final line on the final page of Emma's fairytale. She was the author, but Manny and I took it upon ourselves to see it through to its end, review all of its content, and publish it for the world to see. Nothing else mattered except being there with one another, my arms wrapped around him, his arms wrapped around me. A surge of images rushed through my head: the orphaned baby in the final row of manmade cribs, our flight back home to the States with each other, teaching him how to throw a baseball in our backyard, and our overseas adventure to Greece.

I slung my arm around his shoulder, taking the first step towards the entrance of the store. I often forgot just how tall he was, even at the age of thirteen. If it were a movie, I have no doubt that the scene would be playing out in slow motion. The curly headed girl had made her way to the checkout counter and was chatting with one of the clerks. Her long, hard stare at Manny's sunflower seedless hands was almost enough to guilt me into turning around and going back to buy them, but our job there was done. The sliding exit doors made way for the two of us, their beeping noise bidding us farewell in whatever path life was going to take us down next. We crawled into the truck, took each other's hands into our own, closed our eyes, and began to pray. "Heavenly Father, thank you for your guidance, your love, and your abundance of blessings over these past few months. Thank you for never leading us astray in this pursuit of honoring Emma's memory. Thanks to you, we're now both able to share in the grace of that angel you put into our lives. We can only ask that you continue to grant us strength in the years to come, learning, loving, and living together as we follow in the footsteps of your very own son. Always. Amen."

Part III

Bzzzz* Bzzzz* Startled yet again, only this time by the heavy vibrations of my phone alarm, my eyelids open wide, revealing everything around me as I'd last seen it only forty-five minutes ago. Pulling myself off the indented patch of grass below the dogwood tree, I turn around, bidding it farewell until my next visit. I take one final look at Emmy's gravestone, mouthing the word 'Always' and blowing a gentle kiss before strolling down the cemetery path and through the thick, rusted metal gates to my new, midnight gray Ford F150. Only ten minutes away from the office and fifteen minutes until it's time to clock in, I jam the key into the ignition and allow the truck's cylinders to rumble once more. Turning the wheel, parting myself from the curb, I gradually press harder on the gas pedal until I reach the signal light, watching it turn to green only a second after my brakes brought my truck to a halt.

Cruising with my windows down, I turn off the nagging music of the radio, focusing on the sounds of cars, birds, and people surrounding me. I veer off to the right at the fork in the road, driving just below the speed limit while gazing at the perfectly trimmed tunnel of trees consuming my car and the little space around it. Taking my final turn into the parking lot, I shift into park, reaching over to grab my change of clothes in the gym bag sitting in the passenger seat. I bend down, pulling the handle by the floor, releasing the seat lock and sliding myself a foot backward, providing myself enough room to slip off my shoes and pants, pulling the scrubs up to my waist and tying them in the same unorthodox knot that Emma had always used to tie her shoes.

I pull off my shirt, tossing it carelessly into the backseat as I typically do, pushing my arms through the proper holes in my scrub top and tucking three pesky chest hairs back into its 'v' collar. I grab my lanyard ID from out of the cup holder, looping it around my neck and clicking the two ends together as I walk towards Gate B. Seeing an elderly woman struggling to get her husband out of his wheelchair and into their assistance van, I run over, putting my hands underneath his arms and helping to lift him into the backseat. She folds up the wheelchair and places it horizontally in the trunk, thanking me for my willingness to help the two of them out. I bid them both farewell, jogging at a brisk pace knowing that my shift is set to start any second now. I fling open the doors to Gate B, taking an immediate right through the double doors leading back to the exam rooms.

I peep into my shared office, asking my female coworkers how their day has gone thus far as I quickly erase all of my junk mail in my email inbox. Clicking on one reading "Order Confirmation," I'm pleased to see that flowers are on their way to Ms. Blair's home as I speak, making me even more excited for our lunch date planned for early next week. I exit out of the internet browser, opening up the system's database and reviewing my patient schedule for the next several hours, clicking "print" and heading over to the printer. I snatch the sheet as I walk out the door, hollering to the secretary out front to send in my first appointment of the afternoon.

I step into the third examination room on the left side of the hallway, plopping down onto the surprisingly comfortable chair and opening up the medical records, charts, and test results of Andrea McNally, an 18-year-old girl who has recently completed her final round of chemotherapy for breast cancer within the past six months. The door behind me opens up and in walks Andrea, alongside her two parents. I know that this appointment is one that they've been worried sick over for months on end, perhaps the final check-up on the status of her almost two-year battle. Their forced smiles don't disguise just how nervous they are, sitting here with interlocked fingers as sweat drips off of their foreheads. "How are you guys doing? It's been a while since I've seen you, but you look great!" I look at Andrea, who smiles more genuinely this time, reaching to the top of her head and running her fingers through her newly grown head of hair. I haven't seen her in several weeks, but I remember distinctly just how upset she was after losing it all during her intensive rounds of chemo.

"I'm fairly new to this whole oncology nursing thing, but I've lived through this fight, Andrea." I kneel down, putting one hand on her knee, the other on her mom's. "I've seen the physical toll that it takes." I look over at her mom, then to her dad. "I know just how difficult it is to see someone you've spent the best years of your life with go through something this awful." Andrea's mom begins to cry, making me feel guilty about the point that I'm trying to make. I hand her the box of tissues from the counter, and she gratefully takes two, blowing her nose with one and using the other to wipe away her tears. "If I've learned anything throughout my time spent fighting this, it's that hope and love will beat your diagnosis time and time again. The unmitigated support of your family and friends is better than anything we can put into your body to help ward off the spreading of the cells. Cancer should never take away more from you than what it gives you."

Andrea, now crying, leans over to her dad, tucking her head into his chest as his own eyes begin to water. I stand up and return to the computer monitor, again reading the doctors' notes and assessing the results of her last check-up. "Sweetheart," I spin back around, the family's attention now staring holes through my soul, their anticipation and fear eating me alive, something I still haven't fully grasped in my few short years in this job. "I've read over the reports from your final test, and everything looks as if our prayers have been answered. You're cancer-free, Andrea."

The three of them erupted in tears, flinging their arms around one another, finally having summited the highest peak of their lives. I turn my head so they don't see the tears of joy welling up in my eyes. I click out of the computer program and pull out my daily schedule from my back pocket to see what room I have to be in next. As I walk over to the other side of the counter to retrieve Andrea's file folder, I hear the first spoken words other than my own pierce the air and jolt through me straight to my heart. "It's over. It's finally over." Her father coughs, wiping his face with his sleeve. Andrea lifts her head, looking first at her dad, and then at her mom. "Always," she said, lowering her head in relief that the darkest of her days were finally in the rearview. One lonely tear breaches the walls of my tear ducts, rolls down the upper part of my cheek to the bridge of my nose and falls onto my light-blue scrub shirt, leaving a single, almost unnoticeable drop. I smile, turn the door handle, and let it close behind me without

making a sound.

Printed in Great Britain
by Amazon